# HIS CAT

# AND

# OTHER STRANGE TALES

## DAVID POLLARD

*This is for Glynnis and John Fullick – Good and Generous Friends*

**BY THE SAME AUTHOR**

**ALSO PUBLISHED BY AMAZON**

The Alienation of Ludovic Weiss

**PLAYS PUBLISHED BY LAZYBEE SCRIPTS (www.lazybee.com)**

Can Malone Die?
Aspects of a Betrayal
Clause Fourteen
Illusion/Delusion

# CONTENTS

4

# HIS CAT

Enid stood on the doorstep with the key in her hand, oddly unsure of her next step. The old, familiar feelings of anxiety churned inside her.

But why? The old sod was gone wasn't he? He was good and dead, rot him – she had made sure of that. The undertaker must have thought she was truly bereft when on the morning of the funeral she had burst into the chapel of rest demanding to look upon the face of her departed husband one last time. She had stayed too, until the very last turn of the very last screw in the mahogany lid.

Later, in the crematorium she watched avidly with fixed gaze as the coffin slid through the curtains and into the furnace she knew was behind. Even then her gorge rose at the thought that he might rise up at this last moment and still be living.

But no! He was dead and burnt to ashes. So why was she standing here trembling and not dancing, not singing an anthem of joy as she had promised herself?

Training, she said to herself. Or rather, long and bitter experience. Her mind remembering all the times she had lingered on this doorstep wondering what was waiting for her on the other side of the dark varnished front door. Was he in? Had he been drinking yet? Had he drunk enough to be belligerent, to find fault, to assert himself, as he would put it? Had he had more than that? Was he already comatose, a cigarette smouldering between his fingers as he dozed in his armchair. Or was the volcano dormant and would she spend all evening waiting for the inevitable eruption.

She shook herself. She told herself not to be foolish. She reminded herself that at last the day of liberation had dawned. She was on her own now. She could do as she pleased.

She offered the key to the lock with still palsied fingers. She clicked it open and pushed the door wide.

The house was silent except for the bass ticking of the grandfather clock. His clock. She hated that clock and it would soon be no more. She smelt the dust in the dry air.

The house was empty. Empty except for a familiar black form curled on the second step up the staircase. The form uncurled, stretched itself languidly, arched its back and hissed at her. His cat!

His cat. The animal had never managed to acquire a name of its own – it was simply his cat. It was the only living thing, the only thing in fact that the old devil seemed to care about. Even that was a surly sort of affection, grudgingly given and disdainfully received.

The cat in its turn never showed the slightest trace of affection to him or to anyone else. It never purred in his presence, never offered its back to stroke. In fact it shied away from any sort of direct contact and it never curled in his lap. Every evening, however, the beast draped itself over the arm of his chair as he watched television after he returned from the pub or the Conservative Club.

The two of them just sat there glowering at the screen. The old sod would clutch the remote control appropriating dominion over what should and should not be viewed. Enid had to sit and endure endless soap operas of the most violent, argumentative and angst-ridden kind where actors rehearsed a facsimile of her own anxiety filled existence until she stole from the room and went to bed.

On the morning she discovered her husband lying dead beneath the bedcovers the cat had followed her into the bedroom. As she arranged the covers to give the corpse a vestige of decency the cat had sprung onto the bed and curled itself on the lifeless breast of its master emitting a weird keening mew from its throat. It stared at Enid with rheumy yellow eyes, an unblinking and baleful gaze. It hissed violently and showed its claws whenever Enid dared approach the bed. Then when the ambulance arrived it slunk from the room and disappeared.

Now it was back.

Enid hung up her coat and went into the sitting room. The room smelt of him. His chair stood in the usual position before the television set. Enid shuddered at the sight of the stained and faded fabric. She could almost make out his shape where his back had discoloured the material and his weight had formed the cushions. It was like having him back in the room. The chair reeked of him.

She couldn't bear to stay in there. Tomorrow she would do something about the state of the room and that chair would be the first thing to go. She had a mental list and the chair was at the top. She closed the door and went up the stairs to her bedroom.

His cat followed her up the stairs and tried to follow her into the bedroom. She kicked at it and pushed the door to. The cat pushed back. Enid leant against it, feeling the weight of the cat pushing against her. Once more she heard the strange keening mew. She pushed harder and the door closed. Without thinking Enid turned the key in the lock.

She did not sleep well. Images of her past life with her deceased husband troubled her dreams. In the darkest middle of the night she suddenly became wide awake. She lay in the darkness and there came the implacable scratch, scratch, scratching of sharp claws on the other side of the door. Terrified, Enid pulled the covers over her head and blocked her ears and sobbed herself back to sleep.

The next morning she found the cat waiting for her at the bottom of the stairs.

It followed her into the kitchen where she placed a bowl of cat food in front of it. The cat looked at the bowl disdainfully and sniffed at it. It turned it's watery, yellow eyes up at her and bared a fang in silent criticism. Then it wolfed the lot in three gulps, turned its back and left the room.

Later she found it curled up on his chair. It arched its back and hissed as she approached. Enid was sure that the cat had grown somehow. It had always been sleek and well-formed but it now seemed to have put on more weight and lengthened by a few inches. Enid supposed it must have found someone to give it food wherever it had got to.

Enid opened the French windows that gave onto the garden. The garden she was never allowed to touch or change in any way. She grasped the chair ready to pull it out and onto the overgrown patch of grass that was the lawn. The cat leapt at her, claws extended and emitted a high-pitched shriek as it tore at her hand. Enid fell back horrified as droplets of blood bubbled from the wound.

11

Wrapping her hand in her handkerchief Enid steadied her nerves. The chair was going to go. She was determined. And she would deal with his damned cat.

In the entrance hall she took down the old devil's overcoat. Back in the sitting room she flung it over the cat and seized the beast in her arms. The cat flailed about, hissing violently and then dug its claws into the seat of the chair. Enid heaved at the bundle, astounded at the bulk of the animal and the tenacity of its grip on the chair. She braced herself for a supreme effort, tugged at the bundle and staggered across the room as the cat let go of its grip. She flung the bundle, coat and cat together through the open windows. The cat fought its way out and slunk away into the bushes.

Enid dragged the chair into the garden and onto the patch of bare ground used for burning garden waste. She fetched a hand axe from the garage and a small can of petrol kept for the garden mower. Then, with deliberate strokes of the axe, she demolished the chair until she had reduced it to a pile of wood and fabric which she doused in petrol.

She was just about to strike a match to set the whole thing ablaze when the cat leapt from its hiding place and drove its fangs into her calf. Enid kicked the animal away and without thinking grabbed up the axe and hurled it at its retreating rear. The flat of the axe caught it in the flank. The cat pitched over, screamed, scrambled to its feet and disappeared into the foliage.

Throughout the day Enid continued to work steadily, feeding the flames with everything that had belonged to her deceased but unregretted spouse. She stripped the wardrobe of the few clothes he had owned. He had never been one to spend money on such trifles. He had owned few books and fewer papers but what there was went into the flames. His evil smelling pipes and rank tobacco, they too were pitched onto the bonfire. As a last gesture she dragged the clock from the hall, hacked it to pieces and fed it to the flames.

Later that evening, elated but tired, Enid took herself off to bed. There had been no sign of the cat since she had driven it into the bushes but still Enid locked the bedroom door. Again she slept badly, again confronting her old life in her dreams and again she was suddenly awake in the middle of the night.

There it was again, the scratch, scratch, scratch of claws against the door. She lay there in the darkness as her heart pounded and her body turned to ice. The scratching stopped suddenly. Enid lay there hearing her own ragged breathing and the thump, thump, thump in her chest. Then there came a soft, persistent thudding as of a fur clad body striking the bottom of the door. Gradually the impacts increased in power and intensity until the door was shuddering in its frame. Then as suddenly the whole thing stopped and Enid heard once again the keening mew of the distressed cat.

Then there was silence. Enid burrowed under the blankets and wept herself to sleep.

In the morning the cat was there in the kitchen. It kept its distance though, as Enid placed its bowl on the floor. It waited until she had sat down to her own breakfast before it fell on the food and devoured it, as before, in a few gulps before turning tail and disappearing into the house.

In the clear light of day Enid managed to make light of her night-time fears. It was only a cat after all. There was nothing to fear in its antics. Besides today she was going to take another step in her emancipation from her old life.

Enid put on her coat and took the bus into town. She was going shopping – an ordinary, everyday activity that most women indulged in without fear or flinching. Up until now, for Enid, this same errand had been fraught with danger and hung about with foreboding. But not today!

She had had her eye on a new coat for some time. The one she wore was old and shabby, almost threadbare. She had lacked the courage to replace it but now the new liberated Enid marched boldly into the town's department store and selected exactly what she wanted.

She made other purchases, taking her time, savouring the moments. Finally she thought she would have lunch. Nothing grand, just coffee and a sandwich in a nice café, ordinary to most women but wildly exotic to the long repressed Enid.

In the café she looked around her. Here was the everyday ordinariness long denied her. Other women sat and chatted in couples and small groups. A man and a woman shared a cake over their coffee. Two suited businessmen hunched over their laptops.

Just before she hopped on the bus to go home, on an impulse, she went into the town's vintners and picked up a bottle of white wine.

Returning home the old familiar fears assailed her. She bit them down and let herself in. The cat was there, perched on the second step up, but it seemed to have understood its new place in the order of things. It arched its back and glared at Enid but then let her pass up the stairs, meekly following behind her. It watched her from the doorway to the bedroom as she laid out her purchases on the bed then turned its back and disappeared.

Enid cooked dinner for herself and sat, alone, in the kitchen to eat it. Afterwards she treated herself to a glass of wine and sat down to watch a science documentary on the television. She had never indulged in a glass of wine before, always feeling she had to keep her wits about her in case the old devil became violent.

The cat was nowhere to be seen. Apart from the television presenter the whole house was silent. Enid let herself relax and allowed herself a second glass of wine. She watched the late night news and then, feeling pleasantly drowsy she climbed the stairs to her bedroom.

What she saw in the bedroom sent a bolt of fear shuddering through her.

The packages from her shopping expedition had all been ripped apart and the contents spread about the room and torn into shreds. The new coat, her prized acquisition, now lay in strips of torn cashmere on the pillow. She looked about her. There was no sign of the cat, no sign of an intruder. Silence enveloped her.

Trembling she piled the tatters of silk and cotton and cashmere into a heap in a corner. Tears flooded from her and blinded her. She groped her way to the bed and cowered beneath the covers.

The noises started immediately. First came the regular scratching of claws against the wood of the door – faint at first and then growing in intensity. Then the soft impact of a furry body against the door that grew in violence until the door and its frame shuddered on the point of bursting. Finally the eerie keening mewing of a distressed animal that ended in a final agonised shriek.

Silence followed. Enid lay trembling, listening to her own ragged breathing, counting the seconds. Then it started again and repeated over and over again until Enid thought she would lose her mind and until, mercifully, exhaustion overcame her and sleep claimed her.

The next morning Enid dragged herself from bed and examined the heap of wrecked garments and torn packaging. In the clear daylight it seemed impossible that the cat could have been responsible for this mayhem. The intensity of the violence which had been exerted shook Enid to the core. She shuddered in the presence of such naked malevolence and sheer hatred. Surely no animal less than an enraged lion or tiger could have slashed the heavy coat into rags and reduced the other garments to shreds. No domestic cat, even his cat, could have mustered the strength and evil intent. But what other explanation could there be?

She fetched a black bin bag and shovelled the remains into it and put them out of sight. The cat was nowhere about. She ate breakfast and put down a bowl of meat for the animal which still did not make an appearance.

By lunch time Enid's equilibrium had returned. She noticed that the cat's bowl was now empty. After lunch she dozed then continued to clean the house, eliminating the irksome presence of her departed husband.

In the evening, after dinner, she settled down again in front of the television with a glass of wine. By now she had adjusted her perspective on the events of the previous day. Whatever had happened to her new clothes they were after all just so much material. She would go and buy replacements and make sure that the damned evil beast kept its distance. She was lulled by the fact that the cat seemed to have avoided her for the whole day.

Then the cat walked in. It jumped up on the sofa beside her. Enid was certain now that the thing had got even bigger. It must have been at least three times the size of an average domestic cat. It put out its claws and Enid scowled at it. Then, to her amazement, it arched its back, stuck its tail up in the air and offered its back to her, obviously asking to be stroked.

It was hard to resist such an overture. Gingerly Enid put out her hand and stroked the soft black fur. To her amazement a deep rumble welled up from the cat's throat. It was actually purring!

The animal settled down beside her and nestled its body against Enid's thigh. Enid felt the tension in her own body relax.

They sat like that for several minutes. Enid picked up the remote control and switched on the television. The cat stopped purring. Enid selected a channel and settled back to watch. The cat snorted and spat. Enid ignored it.

Enid picked up her glass of wine. As she brought it to her lips, the cat, with mercurial swiftness, reached up a claw and swept it from her grasp. Wine spilled over Enid, the sofa and the cat. The glass hit the carpet and bounced into the middle of the room. The cat slipped from the sofa and deftly kicked it into the corner of the room.

Enid wiped up the spillage and got herself another glass of wine. Again the pair settled on the sofa. Enid took up the remote control and pointed it at the television. Again, in a flash of black fur, a clawed paw dashed it from her hand into the middle of the room.

The cat jumped to the floor and took possession of the remote control, placing a proprietorial paw on it. Enid got to her feet and confronted the beast. She kicked at it but the cat was too quick and avoided the blow, jumping to one side. Enid bent to retrieve the device. The cat sprang at her sinking its claws into the flesh of her shoulder. By reflex Enid grabbed to cat by the scruff of the neck, wrenched it from her shoulder rending the flesh and hurled it with all her strength against the wall.

Unsteadily the cat got to its feet and snarled, baring a pair of white fangs in blood red gums. Enid turned tail and ran from the room and locked herself in the bedroom.

Seconds later the nightly ritual of terror began. The scratching and thudding and howling continued deep into the night as Enid, blood seeping from her wounded shoulder trembled and wept beneath the sheet.

It is no easy thing to kill another living being. Not in cold blood and without passion. But that is what Enid decided she had to do.

In the morning she climbed out of bed and padded across the landing to the bathroom. She filled the bath and took a large bath towel from the airing cupboard.

In the kitchen his cat was waiting for her. It made no motion towards her, just sat

20

by the garden door watching her as she spooned meat from the tin into its bowl and set it down on the floor.

The cat sniffed at the meat, then turned its disdainful yellow eyed gaze on Enid with what in a human face would have been a sneer on its lips. She had seen that expression all too often. If she still had a scruple about what she was to do next it disappeared in that instant of chilling recognition.

The cat turned away from her and began to wolf the meat. Quietly Enid stepped behind it and threw the towel over it, gathering it to her chest in a single movement. She ran with the squirming bundle in her arms, straight up the stairs and into the bathroom and tipped the animal into the water. She grasped its neck and thrust its head beneath the surface. It fought her but she held it tightly, putting all her weight behind her arm that held the cat on the bottom of the bath.

Air bubbles broke the surface. Then the furry body quivered and went rigid. A few more bubbles then everything was still. Counting the minutes Enid pinioned the lifeless body beneath the surface until she was absolutely sure that all life was extinct. Then she dragged the sodden mass of fur out of the water and dumped it onto the towel.

The corpse was too heavy for her to lift so Enid bundled it into a rough parcel and dragged it, bump, bump, bumping down the stairs and through the kitchen and into the garden, leaving a watery trail behind her.

Shc found a spade in the garage and dug a hole behind some bushes at the end of the garden. It took some time as she wanted to be sure that the cat would be buried deep enough to remain where it was buried. She didn't want it brought back into the light by some itinerant fox where it could haunt her later.

When the hole seemed deep enough and the pile of earth beside her had grown sufficiently high Enid rested and wiped the sweat from her face. She turned to pick up the cat to slide it into the grave and it moved! Enid stepped back aghast. The sodden, furry body twitched again. Then it pushed itself up on its front paws and opened its baleful, yellow eyes.

By a reflex action Enid grabbed the spade and in a single motion brought it down on the animal's head. It squealed and convulsed. Enid hit it again, this time bringing the spade like a blade down across its neck. The head broke from the spine and rolled into the hole coming to rest with its open eyes staring up at Enid and the sneer fixed on its lips for all time.

With a shudder Enid bundled the rest of the corpse into the hole, flung in the blood soaked towel and frantically shovelled the carth on top of the gruesome remains. She found a spare paving slab in the garage and dragged that to the grave-site and settled it over the freshly dug earth. She stamped on it to settle it into the soil.

Exhausted, Enid dragged herself back into the house. She locked and bolted the garden door then sat, trembling, at the kitchen table.

When the tremors that shook her body died down a little she made tea and sat and drank it. The house was silent. Now Enid felt nothing but a great tiredness that swept over her. She climbed the stairs, locked the bedroom door and lay on the bed as she was, fully clothed and covered in grave dirt.

It was already black dark when Enid came awake. She lay in the silence, straining to hear any movement. Remembering the events of the morning she allowed herself a smile. She was safe.

Then, softly at first, it began. The sound of sharp feline claws scratching at the door, scratch, scratch, scratch.

# THE FELLOW OF ST AGNES

## (With a nod of gratitude to the Master, M. R. James)

The Dean of my old college, St Agnes, was an affable fellow. He was much given to regaling colleagues and students alike with tales of mystery and terror over a glass of his excellent port. In fact it was a sort of a tradition with him to entertain small gatherings of the faculty on a winter evening in his rooms. The door stood open to all comers and everyone was at liberty to make free with the decanter and the contents of the tobacco jar.

On just such an evening I was one of the young men gathered around the Dean's fireside. The air was thick with the fragrance of our host's particular mix of fine tobaccos and the port had circulated freely. We were all eager for a tale.

'It is my habit to beguile these chilly evenings by relating a tale or two,' our host commenced. 'Usually these little essays in the workings of the...ahem...unnatural are merely the fruit of my own..er..fertile imagination. Tonight, however, my story is true and I tell it to you as an eye witness; more, as a supporting character in the events that took

24

place within a stone's throw of where we are now sitting in comfort and ease.'

One or two of us exchanged knowing glances and a smile. Was this not a ploy to enliven the palate, jaded with the commonplace, by offering up something with greater piquancy? We acknowledged and approved our host's skill as a teller of tales.

'Yes, indeed, I assure you,' the Dean continued, looking over the rim of his wire-framed spectacles, 'what I now lay before you is the bald truth and not the artifice of the spinner of yarns.'

Thus admonished we settled down as a body to give him our full and unquestioning attention.

'My story concerns perhaps the brightest and most accomplished student that I ever had the privilege of tutoring. I mean you fellows no offence in making this observation.'

How could anyone take offence when enjoying such liberal hospitality?

'Certainly young Clive Upshot was the most distinguished scholar and adornment to this college when he became the youngest Fellow to be appointed to the faculty. I welcomed him as a close and valued friend and colleague. I spent many hours in his company. Our closeness not only sprang from a shared academic bond but was fostered by a mutual enthusiasm for the strange, the unexplained and the plain terrifying. Often he would sit with me, in just such a gathering as is here tonight, sharing a tale or two. As often we would go together in search of new and stimulating materials.'

The Dean paused to refill his pipe. He lit it, drew on it and settled back in a cloud of fragrant smoke.

"One evening as I sat alone, my head nodding sleepily over a volume of Tacitus, I was disturbed by a frantic hammering on my door. I opened to find an ashen faced young Upshot trembling on my threshold. He lurched inside and began immediately to blurt out his story. His words tumbled from him in an incoherent stream. I stopped him and sat him by the fireside and gave him a glass of something to calm and revive his spirits. I stirred the dying embers of the fire and added more coals until a warming blaze had been established."

"When the colour had returned to his face and the trembling of his limbs had subsided I judged that now I should get an understandable story from Upshot. I invited him to tell me what had happened and these, as far as I can recall, were his own words."

"For some time now I have been researching the history of St Agnes church that stands within the college precincts facing onto The High. That church standing on land that was in the original grant at the foundation of the college and being shut up and disused for some generations held a fascination for me. Recently I have uncovered various documents that lead me to believe that this ground was hallowed in the centuries before Christianity and was given over to the worship and veneration of what are referred to as the Old Gods. I feel sure that an orderly and scientific inspection of the ground will yield firm evidence to this effect and I have been preparing a submission to the college authorities to this effect."

"Yesterday evening I had been dining with colleagues out of college and we had sat rather overlong over our port. I regaled my companions with my findings and theories and so the story of St Agnes was much in the forefront of my mind as I walked back to my rooms."

"I must own that I felt a prick of annoyance that my young colleague had chosen to discuss his findings with his peers rather than with myself who had been his mentor through his early career. As Upshot continued with his narrative, however, these feelings diminished to minor irritations."

"I found myself passing that same St Agnes church and felt drawn to make an inspection of the grounds and building notwithstanding that the night was at its darkest and that no street lighting had yet been provided on this stretch of The High. I made a circuit of the outside of the church. The stained glass windows, as you know, had all been removed at the time of Cromwell's Commonwealth and had never been reinstated. Instead, stout wooden boards now covered the window spaces. The front doors of the church were likewise covered in wooden boarding and doubly secured with a thick metal chain and padlock. Similarly, although I came upon a side entrance to the church, it too was firmly secured."

"I toured the graveyard, which was sorely overgrown with weeds to almost the depth of a man's waist. Many of the gravestones were tumbled over and some of the more imposing tombs had suffered the attentions of the youth of the town. I had matches on me and used some to inspect the legends graven on some of the stone tablets. I discovered nothing of significance by this method and my supply of matches was soon exhausted. I did notice, however, that the form of the churchyard was circular in plan. A form that is often associated with the worship of the Old Gods."

"My curiosity being temporarily stemmed and the night air becoming increasingly chill I gave up my inspection, resolving to return in the light of day, and continued on way back to the college. Through the darkened streets, although I heard no footfalls, I felt sure of a presence behind me. I looked back once or twice but could see nobody following me. I supposed that all was my imagination brought on by the late hour and the gloom of the churchyard."

"I turned into the college quadrangle and was about to climb the stairs to my rooms when I heard a thin voice hail me. It was barely a whisper and at first I thought that the reedy sound was a trick of the wind. I looked behind me and saw a figure standing by the porter's lodge. It beckoned to me. I concluded that the figure was one of the college servants who had some message for me. The figure, at that distance, certainly looked to be dressed in a black overcoat and the bowler hat which is the uniform of our college servants. The figure beckoned me again with a degree of urgency. I hesitated still and again, even more forcefully, the figure motioned for me to approach."

"I set off back towards the porters' lodge but as I drew nearer, the figure turned and moved away. I followed and the figure increased its pace, progressing along The High with a spider-like gait in the direction of St. Agnes church. I managed to gain on the black form slightly and could just make out spindly legs and the animal sheen of its coat and hair.

I stopped briefly. I must admit that the pace of this creature was making me breathless. It turned and waved me on insistently before resuming its headlong scamper."

"I followed and whatever I was following turned into the churchyard which I had recently inspected. It disappeared into the shadows along the side of the church where I knew there was a side entrance to the church albeit securely blocked and bolted. Headlong I pursued my leader. The door stood secure as before. I ran to the further end of the church and beyond. The creature, whether man or beast I was now unsure, had quite disappeared."

"Puzzled and much disturbed by these events I could do nothing but turn back once more to the college. I reached my rooms and found my bed. My night's sleep, was not, as you may surmise, a peaceful one."

"This evening I dined in college and went early to my rooms. I was looking over some of the documents concerning the church of St Agnes that I had turned up in the college library when I heard something like a scratching or scrabbling at my door. I opened and found nobody there. I resumed my task and again the sound at my door, something like a rat trapped under a floorboard, came quite distinctly."

"I threw open the door sharply hoping to surprise whoever or whatever was there. Again there was no sign of life. I ran along the corridor to the top of the staircase. Again no-one. I descended and stood in the open quadrangle. There, by the porters' lodge stood the black, emaciated figure of the night before. As before, it beckoned me to follow. It did not wait, however, but set off into the night. I didn't hesitate but followed at once."

"Emerging onto The High I caught site of the scuttling figure a few yards ahead. It paused briefly to be sure I was following and then set off at a pace. Once again I was lead to the church of St Agnes. Once again the figure disappeared along the side of the building. This time, however, the door that had been so securely locked and barred stood wide open. I could do nothing else but enter."

"Inside the odour of centuries, dust mingled with the sweet stink of long extinguished candles, the scent of mouldering books and the decay of fabrics hung undisturbed in the air. I made my way to the nave and stood before the altar. The interior had, of course, been stripped bare; no sacred statuary, no pews and no other adornments had been left behind. I noted a faint but fresh odour of incense but dismissed this as a figment of an overactive and agitated imagination.

31

The place should have been pitch dark but from somewhere a light was thrown to illuminate the space. It is only now that the strangeness of this occurs to me. At the time I gave it no thought at all."

"I found that I had come to a halt on the very edge of an open grave. Or perhaps I should rather say that the cover stone of the grave, which was just in front of the altar, had been pushed aside so that the tomb was half open. I knelt and peered into the void."

"It was just then that I felt the ground beneath me rear up and a dreadful sound filled the emptiness of the church. My head spun and I felt the walls shudder and bend in towards me. The whole space seemed to be pulsating as if the building were breathing with vast retching breaths. I was thrown backwards from the edge of the grave as if a giant hand had thrust against my chest. I'm sure that I fainted because I came to my senses lying by the grave with my legs dangling into that awful space. I dragged myself upright and ran from the place."

"I came straight here, of course. Whatever has been happening, it bears investigation. Will you come back to the place with me? Between us I am sure that we can fathom what is really at the heart of these events."

"Of course I agreed to accompany young Upshot," the Dean continued. "Both of us were sure that delay would only impede our enquiries. We must strike while the trail was fresh. Now how I regret that eagerness. What tragedy might have been averted by delay."

"Nevertheless we prepared ourselves with electric torches and a flask of brandy and set off back to the scene of Upshot's recent nocturnal adventure. At the church we found the side door still standing open. We hesitated and looked about us. There was no sign of any presence other than our own. We entered, cautiously and approached the half open grave. I took a turn about the walls of the building. Here and there, by the torchlight I could make out fragments of centuries old frescoes. The walls were ice cold to the touch and seemed to be covered in a film of green slime."

"When I reached the great main doors of the church I turned to face the altar. I became aware of the noises, the fabric of the building seemed to groaning and creaking as if under a great strain. I saw Upshot kneeling at the graveside and bending into the void as if noticing something of particular significance. Then to my horror I saw a spindly form, covered in sheeny black hair leap from the darkness and bear Upton to the ground. I ran towards the struggling forms with a yell. The

33

groans from the building intensified and with a rending noise I saw the stone pulpit detach itself from the walls and crash down on Upton and his assailant. Before I could reach them the rest of the wall collapsed."

"I knelt beside the fallen stones. Dark red blood oozed between the fragments. There was no question that Upton was dead. A long, thin bony arm covered in black hairs protruded from under the stones. It ended not in a hand but in a single digit armed with a needle sharp talon. It reached towards me, trembled and lay still. I ran from the place and stood trembling on The High. As I watched the whole building seemed to give a sickening upwards heave and then collapsed in on itself."

"I returned in the morning light with the college authorities and members of the police force and fire service. We found poor Upton's crushed form beneath the fallen pulpit but of his monstrous assailant there was no sign. I noted, but did not think fit to bring it to anyone else's attention, that the gravestone had been replaced and now sealed up the tomb."

"The debris of the fallen church was removed and the remaining walls that had survived the collapse were demolished. This was not accomplished without some considerable difficulties and delay. Two of the workmen thus engaged were killed in accidents. Yet others refused to return to the site and further declined to give any reason. Later the college authorities tried to build a new hall and library on the site. The difficulties encountered are too many to elaborate. As you see today, the site has been allowed to become a barren waste land on which only weeds of a singularly unattractive variety can grow."

"So ended the life of one of the most promising scholars that I ever had the privilege to know. His untimely death and the waste of such human potential certainly leads one to question the notion of a benign and ordered Providence."

With these words he took out a large, white handkerchief and gave himself up to a paroxysm of grief. It was indeed too painful for us to see our esteemed and much loved Dean so deeply moved. We stood as a company and silently took our leave.

# SACHA'S TALE

When the woman went out it was a Thursday night. We were both relieved. At least a few hours without being kicked, hounded and shouted at.

Of course she locked us in. We were never allowed out. We got a look at the garden through the patio windows at the back of the house but we were never allowed out there.

We often dreamed of it, you know; being out there, free to wander around.

Mischa, that wasn't her true name just the one the woman insisted on calling her. I was Sacha. Mischa said it was silly to want it, we didn't belong out there, and we couldn't survive. We'd be taken, although Mischa wasn't clear on who would do this taking.

The woman had locked us in to the usual place, a large room with windows high up in one wall. Too high to look out of. Of course, she hadn't left us anything to eat or drink. And it was Thursday and she was always out for at least four hours on Thursday.

I said she probably saw friends. Mischa said she didn't have friends only other people she could boss around. Weak people. Victims.

Mischa said she'd like to tear her throat out and drink her blood. I said then who would feed us and keep us safe?

Mischa said what food she gave us hardly kept us alive. The woman was obsessed with her shape and she wanted us thin like her.

After an hour or so I was really hungry. I started to think...what if I climbed the drapes and reached the window...maybe it was ajar...maybe...It was very high up but I was feeling desperate.

So I jumped up and caught hold of the curtain. Mischa was horrified. Of course the drapes gave way and fell in a pile on the floor.

We sort of gave up hope then and huddled together on the sofa that filled up one end of the room.

The woman would have gone mad if she caught us. We weren't allowed to be on any of the furniture. We had our place and that was it....

Anyway we were safe for a couple of hours or so we thought.

We must have dozed off because we didn't hear the street door opening but we heard the scream when the woman found us curled up on the sofa and saw her precious drapes piled up on the floor.

She was obviously in a bad mood already. She had come back early so maybe her evening hadn't worked out.

Anyway she fetched the stick. It was the one she always used and started to yell at us, chasing us round the room and flailing at us.

Then suddenly she stopped. She dropped the stick and clutched her head, just like she did when she had one of her headaches. She teetered back and forth on her heels, then, with a sort of loud sigh, she crumpled in a heap onto the floor.

Mischa and I cowered behind a chair and watched. The woman didn't move and it didn't look like she was breathing.

After a while Mischa got curious. She always had been the more inquisitive of the two of us. She slunk from behind the chair and poked at the inert form on the floor. No reaction. We looked at each other and nodded a silent agreement. The woman was dead.

Then the enormity of the situation kicked in and both of us started to tremble as thoughts whirled in our heads. This was the end of the world. Of our world.

We clung to each other and curled up on the floor beside the corpse. Eventually sleep took over, blotting out the horrific consequences of what had happened. We might starve...die of thirst...be blamed...be taken!

When we woke up the body of the woman was still there. It hadn't moved an inch. We both instinctively backed away from it, getting as far away as the walls of our cell would allow. Then we sat there looking. I whimpered and Mischa cuffed me.

Well Mischa had got her wish,the woman was dead. But what was going to happen to us?

Light came through the windows high up on the wall. Dawn was breaking. We were both starving by then and dying of thirst. There was a vase of flowers on a table and we sipped from that but even as we did we knew it wouldn't last.

Maybe someone would notice the woman's absence and call round...find us...and the corpse...But nobody ever did come. We knew that. So why would anyone come now?

Through the rest of that day and into the evening we tried various ways to escape; jumping up to the high window, prying at the door. That didn't work of course; the woman was always locking things. She seemed to have an obsession about closed doors. When we weren't trying to escape we huddled together and slept or sat just looking at the body.

We lost track of time, maybe two or three days had passed. I know we heard the thump of mail being delivered a couple of times. By then we were famished and getting weak.

We sat looking at the corpse in the grey light of another dawn. We had avoided going near it until then but now Mischa went over to it and poked at it. The stiffness of death had gone away. The flesh looked pallid but was flabby and yielding. Like it was trying to slide off the bones.

Mischa backed away and looked at the dead woman, her head on one side.

Then Mischa said:

'I'm going to do it.'

I knew what she meant and my gut recoiled. I felt the bile rise in my throat.

'You can't' I whimpered.

'Why not? What's she to us? Then and now?'

Mischa seemed to know what to do instinctively. She bent over the body and bit deeply at the throat, twisting and turning her head as her teeth bit deep into the soft flesh. Eventually blood seeped from the wound and Mischa released her grip and lapped at it.

She looked at me.

'What are you waiting for? Don't let it go to waste.'

I shuddered from deep inside. This was something you didn't do. This was the ultimate taboo.

'Drink...drink now.'

I forced myself to join Mischa...forced myself to put my lips to the wound. The warm, salty liquid bathed my tongue. I'd done it...I'd gone back to some primitive state...in one consuming stroke. But it was survival...it had to be done.

The rest was easy.

Mischa tore at the flesh of the throat and we gorged. Then we slept.

Over the next few days no-one came and we gradually consumed the flesh of our erstwhile tormenter. Soon the corpse started to stink but it didn't matter...this was survival. We drank the water in the flower vase...a sip at a time. That's what we did...ate and slept.

Soon enough we were sharing the corpse with grubs and then flies but still it sustained us.

Now though, it's nearly gone. Another meal or two.

I've noticed now how Mischa is looking at me. We used to sleep curled up together for comfort and warmth. Recently she seems to have withdrawn become remote.

She makes me afraid.

# KILLER JOKE

Stand-up, comedy that is – it was the new rock and roll. I liked the sound of that. I wanted some of that.

I did alright...at first. Did some open mike gigs for free and got noticed. Played a few small clubs – dark sweaty rooms that smelled of beer. Learned to handle an audience – deal with hecklers – make 'em listen to me and like what I was saying. I did the Festival Fringe – Edinburgh- well Leith really. No prizes, no accolades but I got myself an agent out of it.

Terry Grimes – not a bad bloke really. Strictly small time of course but then I wasn't exactly big time now, was I? That's my trouble you see – poor self-image. At least that's what my partner used to say. Said it quite a lot actually.

Anyway, Terry didn't promise the stars but he delivered in his own small-time, run-of-the–mill way. I worked regular up and down the country thanks to him. Bigger places now, theatres even, one-night stands all over the place. No roadies though, no tour manager – just me driving myself from town to town in my second-hand Toyota.

Somewhere along the road I got myself a partner. That's what they call it, isn't it – more than a girl-friend and not quite a wife. I've mentioned her already haven't I?

I wasn't home much what with the touring but when I was, Anthea was there. Well, strictly speaking it was her place – a two bedroom flat near Clapham Common.

So that was how I came to find myself, sitting in the back room of a club in a bleak and run down northern town a couple of hundred miles from Clapham. The gig hadn't gone so well – in fact I'd bombed. Like most gigs those days. I suppose I'd ploughed myself into a rut.

So there I was, punishing myself and a bottle of supermarket scotch which seemed to be my only companion on most nights now. Of course I was feeling sorry for myself but I was trying to be positive. Obviously I needed some new material – some stuff that was up to date, of the moment. But how did you do that when most of the time not spent delivering the tired stuff to a room full of bored punters you were driving or sleeping.

Take some time out you might suggest. How could I do that? I had to keep earning or I'd have Anthea on my case and Terry for that matter.

No, I decided – somewhat unhelpfully – what I needed was a killer joke. Something that would rock the punters, get them in fits and wanting more – then I could riff on the theme and build the set from that flying start. Great idea – but where's this killer joke coming from?

That's where the inspiration let me down. I was done in by then. The adrenaline buzz that I still got from being up there in front of an audience had subsided and the scotch had started to fuzz my head. I needed to bed down and get some sleep ready to drive another hundred and fifty miles to the next gig.

I corked the bottle and lurched out into the night. It was drizzling and the only light in the now empty car park came from a street lamp that barely made an impression on the gloom. Avoiding most of the puddles and potholes I made it to the Toyota and climbed in. It felt damp and chilled as I sat there praying that the thing would start alright and hoping that all the traffic cops were tucked up in their beds.

The windows had steamed up in the short time it took me to find the ignition key again, locate the lock and turn the engine over. It didn't start and in the silence I wiped the mist from the side window.

That's when I saw him. Standing there right by the driver's side door and peering in at me. He tapped on the window.

It was in that split second that all manner of panic fuelled thoughts raced through my head.

Was it the law? A mugger? Maybe an angry punter? Had I laid into anyone particular tonight? Insulted someone's wife or girlfriend? Was he coming to sort me out?

I never like meeting my public for just that reason. When you don't get much reaction in the room you do tend to fall back on taunting the audience. And as you'll have gathered this had recently become the backbone of my act.

I kicked myself for not having left sooner and steeled myself for the car door to be wrenched open and me being dragged out onto the rough cinders for a kicking.

But then I got a look at him.

He was a weedy little chap in a dirty mac and a flat cap. He was probably five feet tall but he was stooped over and his stubbled face was pressed close to the window. A homeless guy, I concluded. Looking for a handout. Had he come to the wrong place!

I wound down the window and asked 'What do you want?'

He poked his head through the opening, so close to my face that I could smell his rancid breath.

'I've got something you've been looking for.'

'What's that?' – I asked, but thinking – shit he's not some sort of dealer – I'm not into that stuff.

'For your act – I've got it.'

'What? Come on – It's getting parky out here'

'A killer joke – that's what you want isn't it?'

'Alright – how much – for this killer joke?'

'Not a thing – at the moment. Try it out – you'll see.'

'Alright – I'm listening…spit it out.'

He started 'My uncle was a self-made man…'

It took about thirty seconds and when he finished I just sat there. What he's said was…well, just not funny. I looked at him blankly – 'Is that it?'

'You try it…you'll see.'

I wound up the window nearly taking the tip off his nose, kicked the engine into life and drove off. As I turned out of the car park I caught a glimpse of him in the rear-view mirror just standing in the middle of the bleak and drizzle swept car park, hands in his mac pockets just staring after me.

I soon forgot about the incident and carried on with what I had to do which was the rest of the provincial one-night stands that Terry had set up for me. Then it was back to London and the flat in Clapham which, frankly, was becoming as unappealing to me as the crummy digs I was stuck with while on the road.

True to expectations Anthea was there with a frosty welcome. She had become increasingly dissatisfied with the way we were living and my long absences on the road. I suppose she might have been attracted once upon a time by the potential of a life lived in the spotlight but quite obviously I was going nowhere with a career in show business. Quite obviously – to her – she had backed a loser.

She started in straightway with the recriminations. No, 'Hello, good to have you back. How did it go?' but more of 'When are you going to get a real job? You're running out of time. You're getting past your sell-by date.' All of it hard to take. But all of it basically true.

I switched off and leafed through the little pile of mail and messages that had been waiting for me. A few bills and a telephone message that Anthea had scrawled on an envelope. Terry Grimes wanted to see me. Not, you'll note wanted me to telephone him or drop him an email. No, face-to-face was demanded.

There was no point putting it off and anyway Anthea was just hitting her stride so I walked out and headed over to Terry's office.

Of course there wasn't any good news when I got to Terry's office. I might just as well have stayed at the flat and let Anthea carry on with the lecture. It was just like hearing a very unpleasant echo. Naturally Terry started off on a reasonable level – how did I think I'd been doing, had I been working on anything new? Then – when there appeared to be no sign that I was going to improve things, become more bookable, on my own, he rolled out the big guns.

Things got heated on both sides – as they always did – and then I just saw red!  I don't know why but it just sort of tumbled out.

'Alright,' I yelled, 'if you want something new…something with some pep in it – try this for size. My uncle was a self-made man…'

I'd barely got the punchline out before Terry staggered to his feet, clutching his chest. His eyes bulged and his face sort of flushed blue and then purple. He toppled forward and his head cracked on the desk. He didn't move and I knew he was dead.

The ambulance came quite quickly and the next thing I knew I was standing on the pavement watching the paramedics load a body-bag into the back. I remember thinking that I should have felt something – some sort of emotion. After all I'd known Terry for a few years, we'd shared a few pints and...well...here was another human being...dead. But I didn't feel anything except a self-interested panic. Where would I find another agent?

I smelt him before I saw him. There was a musty odour, like damp books stored in a crypt. It swept over me like a wave. I felt a brush on my sleeve and there he was alongside me – the homeless guy from the car park.

'See. I told you didn't I?' he said, barely audibly. 'It's all under control. You'll be alright. And don't worry...I've got what I wanted.'

He gave me a little grin and melted into the small crowd that had gathered around the ambulance.

There didn't seem much else to do. I went back home to Clapham and Anthea. And then I just hung around waiting but not sure what I was waiting for.

It didn't take long for Anthea to get tired of this. She might have complained that I was always away when I was gigging but the novelty of having me around all day and under her feet soon wore off. And then she resented that it was her who had to get up and go to work to keep the roof over both our heads

I suppose whatever relationship we had had was already on its last legs. We were both fed up with each other.

So that was it – one night about a week after Terry…you know…it all came to a head .I can't blame her really – she'd had a bad day and I'd only just got up – and she started on me. What was I doing all day? Get off my arse and get some work! Use the time to work on the act!

Then the insults – or maybe they were home truths – started to come out. I was idle, shiftless and could do with a bath. Then she overstepped the mark! I wasn't funny! She actually said it! 'I didn't have a comedy bone in my body!' that's what she said.

Anyone would have snapped and I did.

It just came out without even thinking,' Not funny?' I yelled, 'Alright try this for size!' and I started, 'My uncle was a self-made man…'

By the time I'd finished she was already on her knees – her eyes bulged, just like poor old Terry. She made a little gurgling noise in the back of her throat and slumped over. She didn't move and I knew she was dead.

I didn't feel a thing. There was my best friend – my only friend in truth – dead on the floor in front of me and I didn't feel a thing.

Except – when I thought about it later – I felt a sort of lightness – like something unnecessarily troublesome had been removed from somewhere inside me.

I've felt that ever since – that feeling of lightness, a sort of detachment, like nothing really matters.

Once again I was standing on the pavement as a body was being loaded into the back of an ambulance. Then I smelt him – the musty book smell – and there he was right alongside me. He didn't say a word – just winked and gave me a proprietorial grin.

I worried at first that the police might make trouble for me – what with me being present at two sudden deaths in the same number of weeks. I needn't have been concerned – no-one seemed to pay the slightest attention to my part in all of this. Later I found out that Terry had had a long – term heart condition, smoked and drank too much and was a stranger to exercise. As for Anthea – she was decidedly overweight and it seemed that the stress of losing her cool with me had burst a blood vessel. I admit that I chuckled when I heard that.

I hung about the flat for a few more weeks – after all the rent had been paid – then one afternoon the phone rang. It was some guy I'd never even heard of telling me he'd taken over Terry's clients and he was my new agent. Could I come along and see him? He'd just had an enquiry about a gig he thought might suit me.

Would I come and see him? Try and stop me!

It turned out the gig was on one of those TV news quiz things. You know – a bunch of wise-ass comics riffing jokes about the current news. I fitted right in – something seemed to have changed – in me. Smart stuff seemed to tumble out of my mouth unbidden – without effort or a moment of thought.

One show became five and then I was a regular. I'm doing a sitcom now – wrote it and starring in it – we start shooting next week – so I won't be touring for a while.

Of course the little homeless guy still turns up. He was out front tonight. He's no bother, no bother at all. He never speaks and the smell isn't so apparent. He just sits there giving me that grin

What was that little smile then? That shake of the head? You don't believe me. Or do you think I'm some sort of nutcase? That's it isn't it? You think I'm off my head. Alright smart guy...you just try this for size. My uncle was a self-made man...'

# STANLEY'S TIGER

It was a complete mystery why Stanley decided that he needed a tiger for a pet. Suddenly, one day, the idea just crept into his head and stayed there, nagging at him.

He had had a ginger cat of which he had been very fond. It had been a sleek, fat tomcat and the terror of the local mouse population. That is until age slowed it down and it spent the rest of its days curled in a ball under a radiator in the living room only stirring to be fed and to briefly inspect the garden. Stanley still missed that cat. Maybe that was what gave rise to the thought that now possessed him.

When he told his wife she just stared at him coldly for several seconds and then, in the flat even tone she used when there was to be no further argument she said:

'No Stanley – that is not a good idea.'

Strangely, since Stanley would normally have recognised that the topic had now been placed beyond further discussion, he persisted, arguing that a tiger would be no trouble and could easily sleep in the garden shed. His wife shook her head and stated emphatically:

'A tiger would eat you. They have no manners.'

That is where the matter rested until late one night towards the end of November Stanley was making his way home across the common. He had been kept late at the office and had just managed to catch the last train down from town. The air was chill and Stanley's breath formed a white stream as he breathed heavily from the exertion of stepping out briskly. It was not especially dark as there was a full moon. There was no wind and all was still. Then Stanley heard it.

From directly behind him came a deep, rasping panting and then a low, throaty growl. The hairs on Stanley's neck prickled up with fear but instead of bolting, he stopped and stood rooted to the spot. The panting continued as if the breath were being forced from a deep and hollow chamber. Then another low, gravelly growl followed from deep in a monstrous throat.

Stanley clenched his eyes in fear and braced himself, expecting to be attacked by what was obviously some savage beast. A bead of cold sweat trickled down his forehead and over his nose. He waited, tensed, but the expected assault did not come.

Several seconds passed. Stanley opened his eyes. He thought about taking to his heels. Still the heavy panting continued. Stanley braced himself, turned round and saw, directly behind him, not ten feet away, a huge Bengal tiger.

The tiger stood four-square on its paws and regarded Stanley with baleful gold green eyes. It lowered its head and growled again, deep and low, the vibration trembling the ground beneath Stanley's feet. It seemed to him that the tiger was trying to say something. Again, the chest deep growl came. Yes, Stanley heard it distinctly - 'Meeeat!'

Stanley shrugged his shoulders and shook his head, remembering what his wife had said.

'I'm sorry, I've got nothing for you,' and he held out his hand to show the tiger it was empty. Stanley turned on his heels and set off again in the direction of home. Now, however, he could hear the soft pad, pad, pad of the tiger's feet as it followed in his footsteps. When he stopped the tiger stopped too and the bass note of its panted breath filled the still night air.

Stanley turned and faced the tiger again but he didn't have the heart to shoo it away. In fact Stanley was beginning to think that since fate had seemed to throw a tiger in his path it would be curmudgeonly to ignore the hand of fate. Hadn't he always thought that a tiger for a friend would be a fine thing?

'Alright – you can come home with me. But we must be careful until I find the right moment....You understand?'

The tiger seemed to bow its head as if agreeing to the proposed compact and once again the rumbling growl demanded, 'Meeeat!'

Stanley was relieved to find the house in complete darkness and that his wife had not waited up for him. It was quite simple to ease open the front door without making a sound and to shepherd the tiger through the hallway and into the kitchen without turning on any of the lights.

Once safe in the kitchen Stanley checked in the refrigerator for something to give to his new pet but, unfortunately, nothing obvious presented itself. Then he remembered a few old tins of cat food that were left over after the ginger cat's passing. He rummaged in the larder and found them lurking behind some jars of homemade jam.

The tiger made short work of the cat meat and licking its lips emitted a brief belch before once again rumbling, 'Meeeat'. Stanley, looking around in desperation, saw a note on the counter top by the stove – apparently his dinner had been left to cool and was by the microwave oven. He wasn't hungry anyway and so he put the plate down in front of the tiger.

While his new friend was thus occupied Stanley returned to the refrigerator for a more thorough search. His endeavours yielded a pint and half of milk and some steak he hadn't noticed before. All of this seemed to satisfy the tiger, at least temporarily. The beast lolled on its side, yawned luxuriously and seemed ready for a nap.

'Oh no! You can't just stretch out in here. What if she comes down in the night – my wife I mean...? She can't see you yet – got to keep you out of sight....'

Stanley looked about desperately for some place to hide the tiger. The garden shed? No, too cold at this time of year. Under a rug in the lounge? No, ridiculous. Then he thought of the cupboard under the stairs. No-one looked in there from one year's end to another – just the place until he found somewhere more secure.

Stanley grasped the tiger's rump and tried to lever it up onto its feet. He just got another growl and a lash from the tiger's surprisingly whippy tail.

'Look,' Stanley pleaded, 'you've got to stay out of sight. My wife cannot see you until I've explained things to her carefully. You'll have to stay in that cupboard for tonight. You'll be very cosy, I assure you.'

It looked as if the tiger shrugged its powerful shoulders in an 'Oh well, if it keeps

57

you quiet...' manner. Then with a grunt it got to its feet and padded over to the cupboard and let Stanley open the door.

The next morning Stanley was up very early, aiming to sneak out of the house with the tiger before his wife was about. There was a moment of tension when his wife stirred and asked blearily what he was doing but Stanley sent her off to sleep again with a few murmured platitudes about having to get to the office early. Silently he coaxed the tiger from the comfortable pile of newspapers and cardboard it had made into a nest and silently they slipped out into the early morning mist.

On the journey up to town Stanley was pleasantly surprised at how few people seemed to be taking the train when his usual experience was one of jostle and crowding. In fact he was most gratified to find that he and the tiger had a whole carriage all to themselves. Similarly, on the walk to the office, the throngs of people who always seemed to be getting in his way as they wandered about with phones clamped to their ears or their eyes glued to newspapers or small electronic devices, now parted magically before him allowing him a clear and unimpeded path.

They stopped briefly at a fast food bar and Stanley bought a dozen hamburgers, guessing rightly that the tiger would be wanting some breakfast. The tiger settled beneath Stanley's desk and devoured the meal, grunted and was soon asleep.

At some time during the morning Stanley was called away from his office. On his return he was, at first, somewhat disturbed to find the tiger sitting up behind his desk with an obvious look of satisfaction on its face. His mild perturbation turned to panic stricken horror as he noticed the hank of blond hair on the filing cabinet, the blue shoes tumbled on the carpet and the fragment of a grey skirt draped over the corner of the desk.

The tiger licked its lips with a quick flick of its delicate pink tongue. Elsie! It had eaten Elsie!

Stanley stood aghast and took his head in his hands. What was he going to do? The tiger had eaten the book-keeper! Someone was bound to notice!

Then Stanley began to think. If he could just make sure that someone was at Elsie's desk no-one would pay any further attention. He could catch up on her work later, when everybody else had gone home. Maybe get in a temp to cover the rest of the week. But where could he find someone to occupy the desk just for the rest of the day?

Thinking it through, he paced up and down in front of his desk. At the filing cabinet he idly plucked at the hank of blonde hair. It was a wig! So Elsie wore a wig. He looked from the wig to the tiger and the plan took shape.

It was the work of an instant to fit the blonde wig over the tiger's head. The animal didn't seem to mind at all and seemed to be quite content to be led out of Stanley's office and installed behind Elsie's desk.

Harris, who occupied the other desk in the outer office looked up briefly and then went back to the thick file he was reading. Stanley piled a few files around the tiger in a vague attempt to disguise the fact that in Elsie's place now sat a very large, russet, black and white striped cat. He motioned to the tiger to stay put and returned to his own office and collapsed into his chair.

It looked like it was going to work!

At lunchtime Stanley went out to the local pub for a sandwich and a small whiskey to steady his nerves. It had, after all, been a very trying morning. On his return to the office he knew instantly that something was amiss.

Harris was not at his desk.

Harris never left his desk. He sat down at 9 o'clock, opened the first bulky file from his pile, hunched over it myopically and read, making copious notes. File was succeeded by file as the day progressed. At regular intervals a boy from the post-room delivered yet more files and took away those that had already received Harris' attention. Then, sharp at 6 o'clock, Harris closed the file currently under his gaze, put on his coat and trilby hat and left the office without a word.

Now, Harris was not at his desk. But there were his horn-rimmed spectacles placed on the edge of his desk.

With mounting panic, Stanley followed the trail of debris that led to his office. First there was Harris' pipe, casually cast on the floor by his desk. A pair of pin-striped trousers was next, one leg ripped off at the knee. Harris' shoes stood, neatly side by side just outside the door of Stanley's office. Inside the tiger had reoccupied Stanley's chair, the same smug look of satisfaction on its face as its tongue licked its lips.

Losing Elsie was bad enough but Harris would really be missed. He got phone calls from the outside world. Customers wanted to speak to him. Then there was the post-boy bringing the new files every couple of hours. He was going to be missed very soon.

Stanley knew he needed to buy time but what could he do? Disguising the tiger as Elsie had seemed to work and now without Harris around that ruse was no longer required. So why not promote the tiger to the role of Harris.

In a tremble Stanley rushed around gathering up Harris' glasses, pipe and trilby hat. He also found Harris' waistcoat abandoned in a wastepaper basket. He fitted the glasses over the tigers face and dangled the pipe from the corner of its mouth. Harris hadn't had a wig so Stanley jammed the trilby hat onto the tiger's head instead. He led the tiger to Harris' seat. Then, as final flourish, he draped the waistcoat like a shawl over the beast's shoulders.

To Stanley it all looked quite effective. He was sure that no-one would pay enough attention to notice – at least for today. Then tomorrow...well he would think of something. With a sigh of relief Stanley sought refuge in his office and shut the door.

Towards mid-afternoon Stanley's phone rang. It was the chief's secretary. The chief wanted to see him right away.

On his way out Stanley noticed that the tiger was no longer at Harris' desk. In fact the whole outer office was completely deserted and the door stood ajar.

When, a few minutes later, Stanley entered his superior's office he was not a bit surprised to find the tiger comfortably installed behind the broad expanse of the rosewood desk. Around the room were the tell-tale signs with which Stanley was becoming gruesomely familiar.

The tiger fixed Stanley with a gold green stare and licked his chops. Once more Stanley heard the low rumble of growl starting in the animal's chest, 'Meeeat!'

****

Stanley's wife opened the front door to the insistent scratching as of a large tomcat wanting to be let in. She looked down at the tiger. It still wore Harris's trilby hat and glasses. The pipe dangled from its lips. After a fashion it also wore Stanley's raincoat – one paw being thrust into a sleeve and the rest of the garment swathed toga-like about its flanks.

'Well – you had better come in,' a note of resignation tempered her usual arid delivery.

The tiger looked at her quizzically.

'If you are going to stay you must understand the rules,'

The tiger put its head on one side, listening intently.

'You must hang your things up properly and not strew them around the house. And no dirty paws in the lounge.'

The tiger seemed to nod in acquiescence then rumbled from deep inside it, 'Meeeeat!'

'Oh no. There's the whole common out there for that sort of thing. I'm sure you'll find plenty to your taste after dark. But be in by

63

ten. And don't bring any snacks back for later.'

The tiger growled softly and started to purr.

# A TRICK OF THE LIGHT

I had known Harris for more than twenty years.

He was solid. That's what they said about him in the department. Solid - a safe pair of hands. And they were right. I had never known anyone as unflappable and dependable as Harris. With Harris there was never a crisis – he was all cool competence – no emotion, no histrionics. He was solid; solid like an oak tree.

We had never been particularly close. We were colleagues rather than friends. Of course we had stopped off for a drink after a late night at the office from time to time and then Harris had disappeared into the Underground, on his way off to his flat in Pimlico and I had jumped into a taxi for Waterloo.

Harris shared his flat with his wife, Polly. There were and had been no children.

I had never thought of Harris as being a lover of the countryside. As far as I knew he spent all the time he was away from the office in Pimlico or in the collection of interconnected villages we call London. With Harris there were never any Monday morning tales of weekend expeditions to the country or accounts of holidays spent...anywhere.

That is why I was doubly surprised when Harris retired and he and Polly took themselves off to a secluded place in the West Country and when – shortly after that barely credible event – I received an invitation to spend a weekend with them. I was intrigued to see Harris and his wife in their new surroundings and naturally, therefore, accepted the unexpected invitation.

I drove down and on reaching the small town that lay closest to Harris' new home I was suitably impressed by his choice. The place was a market town surrounded by rolling green countryside and the neat, cultivated patchwork of fields so typical of our English countryside. The main street featured the usual old coaching inn, another couple of public houses, an antique shop or two and a town cross. At one end a parish church of Norman features surrounded by a well-kept churchyard blessed the place. It was all neat and tidy and sleepily peaceful.

Harris' house was some miles beyond the town, along a lane off of the main road. It stood alone, surrounded by gardens. It was a charming residence, built of the dark brown-red bricks typical of the area, under a red tiled roof. Behind the house lay a substantial and ancient forest which seemed to clasp the house and its grounds in a warm embrace.

Polly greeted me at the door and seemed almost relieved to see me. Harris emerged from the parlour and gave me welcome. There were cups of tea after the journey and I was shown to a bright guest room with a view to the rear over the precisely trimmed lawn and to the forest beyond. I noticed that there was a well-trodden path that lead straight from the back entrance of the house to a gap in the trees and thence into the depths of the woodland.

Once I had arranged my things and returned downstairs, Harris seemed eager to show me over the house and this tour lead naturally to an expedition across the lawn to the forest beyond. Polly protested that darkness was beginning to fall and that the visit should be postponed until the next morning. Harris persisted and I felt that for Polly there was more to her reluctance to venture towards the trees than the simple onset of the night. Her face to me held an expression that I read as superstitious dread, but I told myself I must be mistaken. Despite her reticence, however, Polly wrapped a shawl about her shoulders and accompanied us into the depths of the woodland.

Harris by converse seemed eager to be among the trees and stepped out across the intervening grass and plunged into the forest. Sturdy oaks loomed on either side along with elm, birch and alder. Underfoot there was a carpet of leaf mulch and a tangle of roots and brambles. This could, as I imagined, be a last fragment of the primeval woodland that had once covered the whole country.

We came to a clearing and Harris came to a halt. He looked about him with calm satisfaction. His whole frame seemed to relax as if in silent communion with some invisible presence. By contrast I saw Polly shudder and draw her shawl tightly about herself. For myself I found the atmosphere of the place irksome in the extreme. I am not a nervous man and I would not say that I was overly susceptible to impressions but this place troubled me.

I looked about. Darkness was definitely creeping on. I felt a deep chill and a tremor ran up my spine. I noted the gnarled and twisted branches, the scarred bark. For a moment I was sure that I saw one, maybe two faces leering at me from the half-light. I looked away and when I looked back they were still there. It was the trees themselves. I closed my eyes and shook myself. When I looked again they had gone. A trick of the light, I told myself.

I urged Harris to return to the house because of the cold. I saw the look of gratitude on Polly's face as, reluctantly, Harris lead the way back to the brightness and warmth of the house.

We passed a pleasant evening, with tales of the Harris' doings in their new home and reminiscences and recollections of the office and our mutual acquaintances. I slept well, a dreamless and refreshing sleep. In the morning I descended for breakfast to find Polly alone at the table and Harris absent.

"I hope you will excuse William," Polly began, "it's his habit to visit the forest first thing on rising. I had hoped he would be back by now."

I made suitable noises but was rather struck by her tone of apology. For myself I could find nothing wrong with Harris' habit of strolling among the trees early in the morning. In fact I was rather envious of his freedom. Maybe his wife held to a stricter code of behaviour when it came to receiving guests such as me. I helped myself to bacon and eggs and poured myself coffee at her invitation.

We were silent for a while than Polly seemed to draw herself together as if to make some momentous announcement.

"As a matter of fact," she began, the words tumbling from her, "that is the reason I asked you down here."

"The invitation was from you?" I was shocked and it came out in my voice.

"Yes. Of course I suggested to William that he should invite you here for the weekend but it was I that had a motive."

"I see…" although patently I didn't.

"The fact is that we have no relations. No-one in that way that I can consult. And you are the only friend that William has ever mentioned. I find that I am desperately in need of advice and you are the only one I felt able to turn to."

This was quite a revelation of course. I had never given any thought to Harris's social life; I had just assumed that it was as it was. I was shocked, frankly, to be in the position of his wife's only confidant. I was not sure that I relished the role but there seemed nothing for it but to invite her to unburden herself.

"It's the trees you see," Harris' wife began, "they seem to have become an obsession for my husband. It's not just at the start of the day; he would spend all of the day in the forest if he could. In fact he has several times disappeared to the woods from dawn until dusk and has missed meals thanks to his obsession. I'm sure he would sleep out there but, for now, the conventions of civilised life still have some sway with him."

I was shocked and I recalled my own sinister experience in the woodland the night before. I also brought to mind Harris's eagerness to be with the trees. It did seem unnatural on reflection.

"When did this behaviour start?" I asked

"Almost from the day we moved here. I'm sure that the close proximity of the forest was one of the attractions of this house for William. We had barely settled in before he started these expeditions."

"And they have become more regular and extensive with time?"

"Exactly. I believe he is beginning to neglect his health. And, selfish of me I suppose, I am feeling neglected also."

"Have you consulted your doctor?" I ventured.

"Yes, of course, but he is quite dismissive of my fears. His opinion is that a mania for fresh air and the company of the trees is no mania at all but a healthy inclination."

Privately, of course, I was of a mind with Harris' medical man. Harris was in the fortunate position of having nature on his doorstep and leisure to enjoy it to the full. It must have been balm to his soul after the brutal stone landscape of the city and the press of rushing humanity. I could not, however, ignore Polly's very real concerns for her husband and her appeal to me. I suggested that she might find it useful if I had

71

a gentle word with Harris, although I was at a loss how to approach the matter.

She seemed relieved that I had offered to help in this way. She urged me to seek Harris in the forest right away saying that it was all too likely that Harris might already have forgotten my presence and would not necessarily return either for lunch or to salute my departure.

Accordingly I finished off the remains of my breakfast and made my way across the lawn and into the trees.

I came upon Harris in the clearing where we had stood on the previous evening. A shaft of sunlight now lit up the space with an ethereal clarity. In contrast to the night before it now seemed a cheerful and alluring spot. I did not break in on Harris but stood at the edge of the clearing for some time observing him. He wandered about the clearing from tree to tree. Some he stroked and patted, as if petting a loved animal. Some he bent towards with great respect, others he regarded with the same familiarity one would exercise with friends of long standing. All the while I heard him murmuring indistinctly. He was talking to himself. I could find nothing strange in that. Which of us have not spoken thoughts out loud when we thought ourselves solitary?

I coughed to announce my presence and Harris, with no sign of alarm or embarrassment broke off his discourse and gave me a cheerful 'good morning'.

"Your wife told me I might find you here."

"Yes. As she must have said, I find the woods a source of great..."

"Happiness?" I suggested.

"If you will. Or maybe of inspiration and comfort. I find that the trees call to me. It's where I want to be."

I must admit that Harris' candour quite disarmed me. I knew even less how to represent his wife's concerns to him. I saw no obsession or mania in him.

"It was Polly who wanted to invite you down here you know."

I nodded my acknowledgement of this fact.

"The trees...she doesn't like them. I think she resents them. I wish she could see, or better, experience the benefit I derive from their companionship."

I found I had no words to argue on Polly's behalf. I believed, to my later regret, that it was not my place to intervene between husband and wife. I could find nothing reprehensible or unhealthy in Harris' love of the trees. Quite possibly I lacked the sensibility to discern the true depth of his attachment to the forest. Whatever the case, I let down Harris' wife.

I attached myself to Harris for the rest of the morning and we wandered the woods in silence. At about noon I urged him back to the house where we took lunch. Soon afterwards I took my leave and motored back to my home in readiness for Monday morning at the office.

I never did see Harris again. A full year came and went until a telegram arrived.

"Come at once. William disappeared." And it was signed Polly Harris.

Naturally I felt compelled to honour this summons. I arranged my affairs to take leave from the office and with many misgivings set off to the West Country.

When I arrived I found Polly Harris to be calm but deeply troubled. She explained succinctly that since my visit Harris' expeditions to the forest had become more and more frequent and extensive. He had even slept out on some nights and ignored even the most inclement weather to be with the trees. His self-neglect was also becoming troubling. He allowed his hair to grow to a matted length and never tended the full and tangled beard that grew on his face. Indifference to food and drink was now also a feature of his daily habit and he had become gaunt and emaciated.

Then, about a month before she sent the telegram, Harris had failed to return from the forest. Polly had waited several days assuming that this disappearance was simply the next step in the evolution of her husband's obsession with the forest. She hoped that Harris would eventually emerge from the depths of the wood, even more unkempt and filthy, after a few days. She would then be able to ensure that a proper restraint could be placed on her errant husband.

When these anticipated events did not come to pass Polly informed the local police and the Harris' doctor. Searches were instigated in the local area, especially of course in the forest bordering the house. No signs of the missing man, either living or dead, were found. The police enquiries were increased in scope. Hospitals and hotels around the country were circulated with a full description but no information concerning the missing Harris was turned up. Then Harris' wife sent me the telegram.

Naturally I was at a loss to understand what might be expected of me in this case. If the police with their resources could not find Harris what could I alone do? I suspected that I had been called on in the role of chief, in fact only, comforter rather than a source of practical assistance. Just as I was turning this over in my mind and grasping at straws of inspiration, the doctor arrived having been called in by Harris' wife.

She then explained that since we were the only two who knew of her husband's obsession with the forest we might be successful in divining his whereabouts where the police had failed. She herself had developed a firm conviction as to what had become of him, although she did not elaborate on her belief. She wanted the doctor and me to make one last search of the woods. She was convinced that Harris would have left some sign that the two of us, with our privileged knowledge, might be able to pick up on.

The doctor and I exchanged glances which signified our own disbelief in Mrs Harris' theory but neither of us felt able to convey such thoughts to the woman. Consequently we set off together to carry out our hopeless quest.

Even as we crossed the lawn in the direction of the trees I felt that there had been a subtle change in the relationship of the trees with the house. If anything the trees seemed to have moved closer and in some way to have devoured some of the intervening grass-land. The trees themselves also seemed to have grown taller and their whippy tops inclined towards the house shading the lawn beneath. A breeze had also sprung up, soughing through the leaves.

We reached the clearing where I had observed Harris so many months before. At first glance it appeared unchanged, the trees maybe a little taller, the brambles a little more dense. Then I noticed a couple of saplings, very immature, that I was sure I had not remarked before, standing in the clearing away from the established growths. I looked about me and suddenly there they were; the faces that I had seen on that first evening. I peered at them and was sure it was just the bark and boles of the ancient trees forming the facsimile of living faces. Then I was sure of it, a third face had appeared. It was the image of Harris!

I called the doctor and he joined me. I pointed to the images. He stared blankly into the foliage. There was nothing there.

"Was there something? Did you see anything?"

"No, "I murmured, "it must have been a trick of the light."

We quartered the ground, using the forest glade as our starting point and found nothing. Tired out and muddied we gave our report to Harris' wife. I did not mention the faces in the trees. I felt it would only mislead and give false hope. Once again I had let Polly Harris down.

"So, you didn't find anything new. Such a pity."

I felt that I should at least give Harris' wife some small satisfaction, some token that the doctor and I had really tried to carry out our quest.

"This may be nothing...but have you noticed that the trees seem to be encroaching on the lawn?"

"So, you saw that too. I knew I couldn't be mistaken."

The doctor stirred uneasily and cleared his throat. I continued:

"And I'm sure there was some new growth in that clearing that Harris seemed so fond of. But of Harris, I'm sorry but there was really no sign."

Polly seemed to smile to herself briefly and nodded as if agreeing with some deeply held idea that had been confirmed.

"Thank you for your efforts, both of you. I think I know now. Thank you."

It was all quite enigmatic. Nevertheless I was glad that somehow Harris' wife had drawn some comfort from our efforts. I have to say, though, I was very glad when I was able to take my leave and set off back to London.

In the month's that passed and became years no sign of Harris was turned up. I kept in desultory touch with Polly Harris – Christmas cards and the like, and so, was most surprised to receive a letter from her solicitor.

The man of law regretted to inform me that Mrs Harris had passed away some two weeks ago. He further wished to inform me that I had been nominated by the late Mrs Harris as the sole executor of her will. I was requested to visit the district by appointment and to discuss matters with this legal representative. He also went on to tell me that the late Mrs Harris had already been interred as she herself had directed.

Some days later I stood with the solicitor in the drawing room of Harris' house in the West Country. When he had finished explaining to me my duties under the will he asked me if I should like to visit the grave. I was most surprised, having agreed to his suggestion, when he promptly led me through the house and into the rear garden. He then explained that Polly Harris had expressed a desire to be buried in that same clearing in the woods where I had spoken with her husband some years before.

As he led me across the grass and into the trees I saw at once that the encroachment of the forest onto the grounds of the house had advanced significantly. Just a few more years and the foremost trees would touch the walls.

Polly Harris's grave occupied the central space of the clearing. I noted that one of the saplings I had observed during my fruitless search for the vanished person of Harris now stood at the head of the grave. It had now matured, however, into a healthy young tree, the trunk had thickened and a few sturdy branches extended over the grave. I smiled when I saw that beside it, in the earth disturbed by the burial a small shoot was just starting to show.

I admit that the sight prompted a tear to well in my eye. I looked up and saw distinctly the face of Harris formed on one trunk and beside it the image of his departed wife. It was no trick of the light.

# AN UGLY PLANT

When Tomblin moved into the house he knew he had achieved his own earthly paradise.

The mansion flat had been alright. It had been adequate for the needs of a gentleman in business. He had been very comfortable there but there had been no garden. And a garden was what Tomblin aspired to. It was what his soul craved.

The house was fine of course but what set it aside for Tomblin was the garden. The plot was completely out of proportion to the modest dimensions of the house which although charming was of compact scale. The garden stretched for hundreds of yards on all sides of the place. It was well kept and in excellent order but Tomblin had great plans for it – plans of his own.

He had just finished breakfast on the day after he had moved in. His gardening books were all still in the several chests that had been used to transport them from London. There would be plenty of time to arrange the library during the long winter evenings; now Tomblin was anxious to actually make a start on his grand plans. Then the doorbell rang.

There is always a serpent in paradise and Tomblin was about to meet his own particular snake in the grass.

A weedy, unkempt man stood on the doorstep. He was unshaven and dressed in what Tomblin took for the rags of a tramp except for his green rubber boots. They were shiny and untainted by any trace of mud. A sickly odour of stale sweat, damp earth and last night's beer roiled about him and embraced Tomblin.

'I'll just finish digging over the beds at the bottom there,' the man said, gesturing vaguely in the direction of the bottom of the garden, 'then I'll make a start on the bulbs.'

Tomblin was taken aback. Surely the previous owner – a charming old lady in her eighties – had explained the new situation to this person – who he took to be her erstwhile gardener. Tomblin was set on having the garden to himself. He had no need and no desire for help in any aspect of the garden. It was his domain.

'A cuppa tea would be nice...in about half an hour. And a few biscuits. She always gave me tea...and a few biscuits – bourbons...I like bourbons.'

Tomblin found his voice and blurted, 'Didn't she tell you?'

'Tell me what?'

'That your services are...er...are no longer required.'

'What's that?' The man's voice raised in pitch slightly

'I don't need a gardener....'

'But I bin doin' her garden for....

'I'm sorry....'

A silence descended that seemed to Tomblin to last for an age. He rummaged in his pocket and thrust a ten pound note into the man's hand and shut the door.

Unnerved by the encounter Tomblin had lost his appetite for making a start on the garden. He watched through the dining room window as the man trudged away down the lane that led into the village and then set about unboxing his books.

By the next morning the incident with the now ex-gardener had receded from Tomblin's mind and he was calmer. He made a start on the garden. Nothing too radical at first, just simply taking possession of the place and making it his own. He pottered about in the sheds, arranged the tools to his liking and noted some things he needed to buy when he was next in town.

Tomblin liked routine. He set about establishing one for himself now that he was properly moved out of London and master of his own time. He set aside every Wednesday morning to go into the town and get provisions for the week and to visit the bank and the post office and take care of his administrative chores. By lunch time he was feeling virtuous and thought to reward himself with a drink at the local pub.

Tomblin was by no means a drinker but he enjoyed a pint of beer. He had always aspired to have what he had heard called 'a local'. A pub where he was known, always acknowledged with a friendly greeting, his favoured brew drawn ready for him on the bar. At his first visit to the 'Royal Oak' Tomblin was favourably impressed until glancing round the bar he caught sight of the erstwhile gardener hunched over a half empty pint glass. The reek of the man seemed to reach across to him. The man looked up and grimaced spite.

Tomblin took a seat at the corner of the bar, turning his back on the unwelcome apparition and ordered his drink. He seemed to feel the man's eyes on him and it was a most unwelcome feeling. A while later, mercifully, Tomblin heard the scraping of furniture and clunking of the door that signified the departure of the man. He was alone in the bar with the landlord who was bent over the local newspaper which he had opened on the counter.

"That man," Tomblin started, "does he come in here much?"

"That's Roger," the publican replied seemingly eager to have someone to talk to, "he's in here most days and nights. Don't know where he gets the cash from. Still he's no trouble. He just sits and drinks. Never says a word to anyone."

"He does gardening, I understand?"

"Ah, you must be Mr Tomblin. I hear you let old Roger go. He was having a bit of a moan about it the other day."

Tomblin was struck by how such a silent man by the landlords repute could have 'a bit of a moan' about losing a job. The publican was continuing;

"He was always up at your place, looking after the old lady's garden. Treated it like his own."

"Well it's my garden now," said Tomblin, half to himself.

Tomblin made a start on his garden that afternoon. The weather was kind, dry with just a hint of the heat to come in the summer months. Three days passed in this peaceful occupation. It was on the morning of the fourth day that another unsettling encounter took place.

That morning Tomblin was greeted with the sight of Roger already at work with a spade on a bare bed towards the top of the garden. Tomblin chased him away with harsh words and threats of the police should he ever return. Roger stumped up the garden path and turning over his shoulder seemed about to utter some imprecations. Then he seemed to think better of it and left without another word.

When he next visited the top of the garden Tomblin was appalled to see that some sort of plant had erupted from the ground where Roger had been digging. It was most definitely the ugliest plant that Tomblin had ever seen. It already stood at knee height. A thick green stem covered in vicious looking black thorns thrust up from the ground. From this stem a sickly cream, viscous liquid suppurated and dripped over the thorns and stem, pooling on the earth at the base. Sparse bunches of diseased looking leaves, deeply serrated and clenched like an arthritic fist hung from the stem. The whole hideous thing was capped by a crown of thin, tentacle-like whippy stalks, each tipped with a bruise purple bract

Tomblin was seized with revulsion. He grabbed a spade and chopped at the base of the plant severing it from the root in a single stroke. He tossed the stem onto the weed pile that was waiting to be burnt. Furiously he dug out the roots and added them to the pile.

It was some little time before Tomblin visited this particular area of his garden again. He was horrified to find that the ugly plant had somehow survived his attack and had now established itself in the weed pile. Indeed its ill treatment had seemed to encourage its vigour. It was now three feet tall and the whippy tentacles had become thicker and more supple.

Tomblin went to fetch the spade. When he confronted it again it seemed to him that the plant had taken on an aggressive stance in anticipation of an attack. It seemed to crouch as if about to spring at its adversary. Tomblin, unnerved, edged towards it. Suddenly a thick tentacle was thrust towards him and seized him by the wrist. Tomblin felt himself being steadily drawn towards the plant. Just in time he remembered the secateurs he always carried at his belt. His free arm looped down and caught up the weapon. A sharp upward movement and he had severed the sappy limb. The residual piece slithered from his wrist and shrivelled at his feet.

Tomblin picked up the spade from where it had fallen and swung it at the green and thorny stem of the plant. He severed it in two and as he did so the plant let out a piercing screech. Everything went still. The birds stopped singing, the wind sighing in the trees dropped; there was no sound except the blood pounding in Tomblin's ears. He struck again at the base of the plant, severing it from its root.

He took a fork and parted the pile of weeds which this ugly plant had colonised. The roots had tangled themselves in the discarded vegetation and seemed to be drawing nourishment from its victims. At the bottom of the pile there lay a pool of sludgy, green matter, the detritus of the plants feeding. Tomlin hacked at the roots until he was satisfied that the whole thing had been destroyed.

That same week Tomblin went into town on the Wednesday as was now his habit. In the same way he visited the "Royal Oak."

"Pity about old Roger," the publican who Tomblin now knew as Tony confided. "In the hospital, he is. Lost his leg. His own fault really. Never looked after himself. Had an ulcer on his shin. Gangrene set in."

The plant was back in a few days. It seemed to have lost some of its vigour and drooped to the right as if somehow shorn of support on its left hand side. Tomblin didn't hesitate; he'd already got the spade handy. It was the work of moments to vanquish the unwanted and invasive plant.

That week Tony at the "Royal Oak" had more news of Roger:

"He's out of hospital, you know. They had to take off his other leg. Poor devil's in a wheelchair."

Tomblin received the news with a pang of anxiety. There couldn't be any association between the plant, or what he had done to it and the erstwhile gardener's condition. Could there? Contrary to his habit he ordered another pint and drank it slowly as he reflected on the strange and coincidental nature of life.

It was inevitable that the plant should be back to plague Tomblin. He was now prepared to get rid of it once and for all. The weather had been dry and hot for weeks now and the pile of weeds on which the ugly plant had established itself was tinder dry. Fire, Tomblin told himself that would be the solution to this aggressive plant once and for all.

The plant was obviously suffering. It drooped even more and it leaned over to the right at an acute angle. It made no aggressive move. Indeed the tentacles seemed to flinch away as Tomblin approached.

He fetched his tools and again hacked the plant down to the ground. He checked under the pile to be sure that the plant had not put roots down into the ground and was pleased to see that the only root system had again coiled itself into the other weeds in the pile. Just to help things along Tomblin sprinkled a little petrol onto the pile and touched it off with a match. The flames shot skyward and as the fire took hold Tomblin again heard the squeal of agony on the evening air.

Tomblin looked up at the gathering evening sky as the flames leaped higher. Over towards the town a crimson orange glow lit up the sky, mirroring the fire that crackled in front of him. On the night air he heard the wail of sirens and saw the flashes of blue lights.

When he next went to the small town Tomblin noticed a burnt out building just as the countryside gave way to the paved streets of the town.

"Went up like a torch," Tony was saying. "Poor old devil never had a chance, being in a wheelchair and all. Must have been burnt to a crisp. Same again?"

A little while after that Tomlin sold the house and garden and moved away. He went to live by the sea in house that stood right on the edge of a shingle beach. Behind the house there were open fields where a farmer grazed sheep. Tomlin never touched a spade again. He seemed to have lost interest in gardens. Grass apart, and that was for the sheep, no plant grew anywhere near him. He turned his

back on the land and sat every day looking at
the shingle and the waves beyond.

# PROBE

The probe had travelled many millions of miles in the twenty years since it was launched towards the source of a faintly detected, regular pulse of radio energy. The whole expedition had been an incredible leap of faith by its originators. Some days ago, monitored by the survivors of the original team and their successors who still waited in the mission control room, the probe had entered orbit around a planet beyond the edges of their galaxy and of the collective imaginations of those originators. Their hopes, it seemed, had been fully realised when they saw the first grainy pictures sent back from the probe. They saw a green and blue planet much like their own.

The probe had touched down on the surface of the planet, emerging from the shell-like structure that had been intended to protect it from the potential shocks of entry into the new planet's atmosphere, exactly as planned. This vehicle, known affectionately by the team that built it as 'The Egg' broke apart, releasing the probe which rolled forward on its tracked undercarriage, clear of the two halves of the shell.

The probe was officially known as IEX01 by its creators, however, a programmer with a touch of whimsy had, without permission and strictly on her own initiative, inserted a prototypical artificial intelligence routine into the central processor of the probe. It was intended to provide the device with a sense of self awareness. As a result the probe preferred to think of itself as 'Bill'.

Bill took some readings of the atmosphere and judged the gas mix to be equivalent to that on its planet of origin. It sampled the ambient radiation energy which appeared to emanate from the sun-like object that hung in the sky and considered it was sufficient. Bill deployed its solar panel array and began to recharge its power cells. To achieve a full recharge of the energy systems would require several hours. Bill set a timer and closed down all other processes.

When the timer elapsed Bill woke up, folded the solar panel array into its housing and looked around itself.

The probe's programing required it to perform a series of experiments and observations before proceeding from the landing site. An auger was extended from the body of the machine and samples of the material forming the surface of the planet were gathered and analysed. Likewise several rocks that stood within reach of the probe were gathered in and their content inspected.

Fortuitously the probe had landed beside a stream of clear liquid. Again samples were drawn and analysed. Temperature readings of all materials and the surrounding atmosphere were taken. Finally Bill captured numerous visual images of the surrounding area. All of this information was processed and packaged into a stream of data which was, the scheduled time having arrived, transmitted into space to ultimately arrive at the probe's point of origin.

There were now some hours before the next scheduled time for the probe to send back information to the command centre. Bill folded his various tools into the protective shield that surrounded his mechanisms and trundled off to explore.

The probe traversed open grassland beneath a blue sky. It came to a stand of trees and paused to gather and analyse plant samples then trundled into the woodland.

Bill's motion sensors detected movement at some distance. The probe paused and signs of motion came again but stronger. Whatever was moving over on its left flank was approaching it. Bill backed into the shade of a group of tall trees, and became stationary behind a clump of tall ferns. It extended the lens of its scanning apparatus.

A creature came towards the probe's place of concealment. It stood erect on two pylons and moved forward with a smooth movement of these pylons. Its progress was tentative as if wishing to make as little impact on its surroundings as possible. The creature stood about six feet tall. At either side of its body the probe identified what it took to be three arms ending in claws. On adjusting the focus of the visual scanner it became clear that one of these arms was in fact a stick-like object that was carried rather than attached to the creature's body. The probe recorded several images of the creature and cached them for future transmission.

The creature did not notice Bill behind the clump of ferns and moved past and on into the forest. Responding to his mission programming Bill allowed the creature to extend the gap between them to several yards before following silently in its tracks.

At the same time the probe scanned the surroundings for signs of other such life forms. At a point some fifty yards ahead of the first creature Bill noted another moving object.

The creature came to a halt and itself appeared to be scanning for what lay ahead. The probe again captured images of the animal. On inspection the creature looked to be covered in a mixture of skins. An extension like a tail seemed to be hanging from the back of its head which itself was covered in a thick brown fur. A smooth tawny layer covered its upper body and the pylons that supported the whole frame were likewise wrapped in a coarser, brown and hairless skin.

One of the original creators of the probe had envisioned IEX01 making contact with life forms at some point in the mission. To equip it for such an eventuality the team had spent many hours debating the best method for the probe to establish such contact on friendly and non-threatening terms. Informed by their own culture the team had designed a sonic vocalisation to be used when encountering these putative life forms. Bill now brought this into play.

The creature displayed every sign of fear and readiness for flight when Bill released the high pitched screech. Other life forms that had been invisible in the tree tops took to the air or scampered in all directions. The creature turned to identify the source of such a deafening and painful sound and saw Bill standing just a few yards behind him. It stood transfixed for several seconds then turned about and fled at considerable speed. Bill picked up a squeal similar to his own greeting emanating from the creature. Encouraged, the probe followed.

It became clear that the fleeing creature was rapidly depleting its energy reserves. At last, near the edge of the trees it came to a halt and, bent double, was gasping in the oxygen and nitrogen gas mix of the planet's atmosphere. Bill likewise came to a halt.

The creature recovered slightly and stood looking at Bill. It raised the stick and pointed it at Bill. There was a flash of light and a loud explosion as gasses and flame erupted from the stick and a missile sped in Bill's direction. The creature lurched backwards and dropped the stick. The missile passed over the top of the probe's domed protective shell.

Once again the creature set off at speed and Bill followed. A few yards further on Bill observed the creature pitch forward and roll out of sight.

The probe trundled forward. Just where the creature had fallen and disappeared, Bill came to the edge of a pit. The earth fell away from this lip into a deep void. At the bottom Bill detected the motionless form of the creature.

At the bottom of the pit Bill approached the creature. A red, viscous substance was leaking from the creature's head. Bill sampled and analysed the liquid. Likewise Bill took samples of the fabrics and skins covering the body, all of which lay over the natural covering of the creature which was virtually hairless and of a pallid grey-white colour.

Bill again scanned the immediate area and again picked up the presence of a similar life form close by. Soon a crashing sound of undergrowth smashing and a large creature approaching reached Bill's sensors.

A face covered in fur appeared at the rim of the pit. The head of this creature was quite different to that of Bill's first encounter. That one, the dead one as Bill had determined by the lack of vital signs, had a flat face, almost featureless apart from the protuberance of its breathing tube. The new comer's face was pointed and the open jaws displayed a healthy array of serrated calcium material.

Bill tried his greeting vocalisation on the creature. It seemed to enrage the creature rather than sooth it. A great body leaped into the pit and seized Bill around his circumference. The probe flew through the air for a couple of yards before landing heavily on a fallen tree trunk. This in itself was sufficient to tear the outer skin of the probe and disconnect several critical components.

It appeared that the probe's assailant would not be satisfied with this first demonstration of its powers of destruction. Bill was again picked up bodily and smashed to the ground. The bear then set about dismembering the remains of IEX01 and scattering them around the pit. Finding the remains of the probe not to his liking the bear then turned his attention to the dead body of the trapper.

The shift operations manager stared at his blank screen. It was over two hours since the probe had been scheduled to transmit the results of its explorations. The only possible conclusion was that IEX01 had experienced a catastrophic system failure. There would be no coming back for the probe. It was dead without a doubt. He would have to report this to the Mission Controller. At least they had got some enticing information in the few hours that IEX01 had managed to stay alive on the distant planet. Surely there was enough to encourage investment in a second mission. He might still be alive when it landed on the remote world.

He ran a three fingered talon to ruffle the feathers on top of his head. It was going to be a difficult conversation. Better to impart the bad news face-to-face. He spread his wings and glided down from his perch.

# AT THE CROSSROADS

Robert was feeling fine, mighty fine. The woman he had spent the afternoon with had even fed him a hot meal before she pushed him out the back door. She was standing over there right now, giving him a little smile as she stood in the corner with her girlfriends.

That was one fine woman. She was almost pale enough to pass for white and she had a sassy, upfront look about her. Looked you straight in the eye. That Henry Dundy was nothing but a fool. Fine woman like that at home and him out fishing and chugging moonshine with his pals. There he was over by the door, still with a jug in his hand. Should have been home taking care of business, that's where he should have been.

Robert smiled inwardly. He had sure given her what she needed that afternoon. He didn't feel like he'd done old Henry any sort of wrong. It was nothing but a loan after all. He'd be out of there soon as he could hop a north bound freight train. Memphis, that's where he was heading. Then even further north, maybe even get to Chicago.

He still had most of the seventy-five dollars the man had given him in the hotel over in Dallas. They'd recorded eleven sides in that session. There'd been whiskey too. Store bought stuff, in a bottle. The recording guy said it had come across the big lakes up north from Canada. The man from the record company seemed pleased enough. He'd promised there'd be another session next time he came through that way. It all felt pretty good to Robert.

He nestled the guitar to him and tapped a rhythm with his foot on the boards of the makeshift stage. He struck the strings and started another hard driving blues. The guy they called Sonny Boy started in on his harmonica with a wailing complement. A guy he didn't know with a fiddle joined in. Robert felt the power as the feet beat the dirt floor of the juke joint and the musky scent of close packed sweating bodies rose up to him.

Henry handed his jug to a tall skinny black man who stood at his shoulder. The guy was old and looked like a skeleton draped in a shabby black suit. The skin on his face was drawn tight. He looked like a black death's head with the oil light glinting on his smooth and hairless skull. He took a long steady pull on the jug and handed it back to Henry. He looked straight across at Robert up there on the bandstand. His eyes bulged slightly making him look even more cadaverous. He didn't blink. He didn't grin. He just looked; blank and unfeeling.

Robert knew him then. Memories of the night came back to him in a flood as he continued to play.

He'd been down in Louisiana, travelling the Delta country, when he found the witch woman. Or maybe she found him. Afterwards Robert had never had a clear recollection of how he came to be in her sod shack on the banks of a bayou. She stirred from under the blankets that formed a nest in one corner of the cabin. It was hot in there. A pot-bellied stove belched heat and smoke into the room. Outside it must have been thirty degrees in the shade but still the old woman clutched the blankets about her shrunken form as if she were freezing.

"I know what you want," she croaked, "and I can help you get it. It'll cost you though."

Robert held out some crumpled bills, most of what he had. Her claw like hand snaked from the blankets and snatched them.

"Not talking money, boy. Cost you more than money."

She gave Robert a hank of hair bound together with a couple of inky black crow feathers and a bone. She told him what to do.

That night, at the cross roads, he scraped out a shallow dip in the earth and buried the mojo hand. He waited. After what seemed hours in the chill night air he saw a figure coming along the road towards him. The figure resolved into a tall, skinny black man, dressed in a shabby black suit. He was walking quickly with a slight stoop. His face was shaded by the brim of a broad black hat.

The man leaned over Robert and spoke. His breath was thick with the taint of rotting cloth and damp earth. It was the stench of the graveyard.

"You got something for me, boy?"

Robert produced the bottle the witch woman had told him to bring. The man took it and hefted it in his hand. He opened the bottle and took a long pull. He licked his lips and drank again.

"That's good boy. Real good."

Robert started to speak but the man held up a bony hand to stop him.

"Here boy, you take a drink. You drink with me."

Robert took the proffered bottle and raised it to his lips.

"That's right, you drink with me. I know what you want. Least I know what you think you want right now. That'll change. But I can give you what you want now. You know there's a cost?"

The man's tone sent chills through Robert even though he knew where all this was leading.

"Sure you do. You know. Otherwise why come here? You drank with me. You know."

Robert handed back the bottle and the man drank again.

"It's already in you, boy. Just got to let it out. I can let it out of you."

The bottle passed again, they both drank.

"That's sealed. I'll see you again. But not too soon."

The man strode off into the night, the bottle, now half full, dangling at his side. Robert sat watching him go down the road until the blackness enveloped him. Sleep overcame him and when he woke it was dawn and he was soaked in the morning dew.

It took time. Robert was starting to think he had been taken for a fool when all at once it all came together. He felt a new power in his playing and crowds were drawn to him. He played street corners and his hat filled with nickels and dimes. When he arrived in a new town people seemed to be waiting for him and there was always somewhere to play, a bar, a juke joint. And there was always somewhere to sleep afterwards, food, whiskey and any woman he wanted.

Then there was the session in that hotel room in San Antonio, Texas. They'd cut sixteen sides in that three day session. The record company guy had promised there'd be more sessions and he came through.

Robert was sitting on top of his world, and now the skinny black man was back. There was no denying what was going to happen now. Robert finished the number and put down his guitar. He stepped down from the makeshift platform and merged into the crowd standing on the dirt floor. Behind him he heard another musician take his place and the music start up again. He pushed his way through the sweating bodies until he was face to face with Henry Dundy and his cadaverous companion. The scrawny black man leaned in to Robert's face. Again he tasted the stink of the open grave.

"Robert, "the voice not above a hoarse whisper, "I said we'd see each other again."

"It's too soon. I'm not..."

"Ready? No-one is ever ready. But a bargain is a bargain Robert," and a scrawny black hand gripped his shoulder.

"It's too soon," Robert insisted.

"I say when. That's the deal."

Dundy, as if following an unspoken cue held out the jug.

"Take a drink with us. Go right ahead."

Robert took the jug and looked Dundy in the eye.

"What's the matter? That's good 'shine. I know where it came from. You're going to drink with us, aren't you?"

Dundy's tone told it all to Robert. Henry Dundy was not such a fool after all. He knew and he knew the value of his woman. The skinny man reached out and took the jug from Robert.

"Ain't nothing. He just wants to drink with an old friend. That's right Robert?" and he raised the jug to his mouth. He swallowed and handed the jug back to Robert. "You'll drink with me, won't you Robert?"

Sonny Boy was standing at his shoulder. He reached across and took the jug.

"Don't be a fool Robert. Never take a drink from an opened jug."

Robert snatched the jug back.

"Not your business and never take a jug from me again!" and he raised the jug to his mouth and took a long swallow.

He felt the numbness grasp his gut at once. The room swum and he sank to his knees. The music stopped but all Robert heard was the ringing in his ears. A crowd gathered around. Henry Dundy and his companion were not of it. The press of bodies parted. The face of Henry Dundy's woman was the last thing that Robert saw in this world

# IN THE PIT

This is the place. This is it right enough. I never thought I'd be back here. Of course I came back when they reopened the pit after the cave in. I didn't have a lot of choice really what with there being no other work around these parts and you on the way. I always avoided this place though.

Even then it didn't last, did it? There was the strike and the police, all that. All that's in the history books now though isn't it? Coal's not what it was. King Coal they used to call it. Now they tell us burning coal's destroying the planet. It lasted long enough though. When they closed the pit I was more than ready to leave all that behind me. I found other ways to make a living in the end. Turned out it wasn't the end of the world.

Great thing though, what they've done here. Preserved it like. Made a museum of it. Now tourists can come and have a look at the industrial past. And I could come along and show my lad what went on down here.

Yes, this is the place right enough.

He was over there, sitting, with his back against the wall. I said to him as the dust was settling, 'you alright? Still with me?'

He blinked his eyes and gave me that lopsided grin. He didn't say a word. He just gave me a wink. I'm sure he shrugged his shoulders too.

He was like that, your da. Not much to say for himself. Stoic. That was him. Stoic.

We still had some light. We'd only just started the shift so the batteries had plenty of life.

I crawled forward but there was no chance. The tunnel behind us was completely blocked and in front of us just the blank wall of the coalface. Nothing for it but to wait.

I don't mind telling you I was scared. But I put on a brave face for him. I crawled back beside him. 'They'll be here soon enough. They'll get us out. We'll be alright here.'

I sat alongside him and I found that I'd taken his hand. We just sat there. I had my snap and a tea-can. I shared my piece with him and we had a sup of cold, black tea each. I began to feel a bit calmer. I was all in one piece after all. No bones broken. Something to be grateful for.

Then I started talking. I couldn't stop myself. It sort of spilled out of me in a word torrent. I told him, like. About me and Megan...your Ma.

He never stirred but I could swear his grip on my hand tightened. He never spoke.

So then we sat there in the dark. The cold was chilling my bones and I'd started to tremble with it. It was damp too. Your Da, he put his arms round me then and held me close, sharing his own warmth with me.

I suppose I must have slept. Maybe I dreamed too. Dreamed about your Ma, Megan. I know I woke up with tears making grey rivers in the coal dust on my face. Your Da was still there beside me. I heard him whisper some words of encouragement, putting the resolve, the resolve to stay alive in me.

Just before they came he leaned over and told me to look after Megan, our Megan. And to look out for you as well. I must have drifted off again soon after that.

Then we heard them. Down the tunnel. We heard the chink of picks then the sound of their voices.

They told me he had been dead since the moment of the cave in – your Da. His back had been broken you see.

I married her, of course. Your Ma. But you are his. No question of that.

# IN HER IMAGE

Sammy Stein sat at the kitchen table with his second breakfast mug of coffee. It was treacle black and strong, just the way he liked it. Sure the doctor was always telling him that it wasn't doing his heart any good; but what did he know? He was still here wasn't he and he still was doing alright.

Golda, the love of his life, was stooped over the sink, up to her chubby elbows in suds. The love of his life. How could she be anything else after nearly fifty years together?

She'd been a real beauty when she was a girl. Sammy smiled to himself, remembering the girl he had courted. Then she'd turned into a woman, a woman of character and gentle loveliness. Now she was stout and old. Then so was he. They'd grown old together. She was his best friend. She was his Golda.

Sammy remembered sitting in bed on Sunday mornings watching her dress. Sitting there seeing her at the dressing-table mirror, admiring her curves and the soft pinkness of supple flesh. Ach! Such a beauty.

Now here she was deep in the washing up. They had a dishwasher. Nothing but the best for his Golda. Would she use it? No. She preferred to do it her way, the way she had done all her life. If she needed machines to look after her home, to look after her Sammy, than she was done for.

He'd done alright in life, a lovely wife, gracious, a support. She'd given him two sons. When he finished he'd had three shops. Everybody knew Stein's the jeweller. Not bad at all.

The boys had been good to him when he retired. His sons, his son the lawyer, his son the accountant. They'd made him chairman of the board. They'd let him come into the shops when he felt like it. He'd never interfered. It was their world now. His boys had plans. They'd take it forward. They'd build on what he'd established. He stopped dropping in on the shops. He hadn't been by for, what, six months maybe.

They'd been careful for him too; anxious to know how he'd fill his time. They'd wanted him to feel useful, to feel fulfilled. Sammy had known right from the start what he wanted. When the shops had started to do well he had had to come out of the back room where he created such lovely works of art in gold and silver. He missed the creative side of his trade. He knew there was an artist inside him. That was it. He wanted to create beauty again.

The boys had bought him a workshop or studio as they preferred to call it. It was a substantial wooden building and it stood at the end of Sammy and Golda's garden. It came equipped with whatever an artist might need –'just add inspiration', Sammy had joked, as he choked back the emotion the gift had invoked.

That was where Sammy spent most of his day now that he didn't visit the shops. He finished his coffee, gave Golda a kiss on her downy cheek and strolled down to the studio.

For some little while now Sammy had been trying his hand at painting. He'd taken a few classes and his technique was evolving steadily. Just now he was working on a landscape or rather a snowscape. Golda liked snow in pictures. This was for her.

He sat staring at the canvas, brush in hand, pallet ready charged with fresh oil paint, but his mind had wandered back to the lovely girl he had married. Then by a chain of thoughts he was led to contemplate his own position. Where was the young and virile lad who had courted the lovely Golda? Sammy was too much of a realist to feel remorse for lost youth. Would he want to do it all again, recapture his youth and relive it all? No. Not a bit. What really griped his soul was the sheer inability of capturing the essence of youth; of being able to preserve just a few fragments of that golden time. Just to have something tangible to take into the future.

He shook himself out of what was, to the realist in him, a pointless reverie. He pulled his attention back to the canvas in front of him. Just a few moments later his mind had wandered again; back to that image of a lovely girl who had been his Golda. He knew there was no point in pushing on with the snowscape. No point in forcing himself to put brush to canvas. He had to follow inspiration not force it to appear. That was the trick, to let the elusive insight appear unbidden and then follow its lead.

He found his sketchbook under a pile of catalogues and sat down at the studio window. He let the thoughts fill his head; let pictures of his early days appear to his mind's eye. He began to draw, filling the page with small images, images of the lovely girl that had been Golda. There was Golda sitting, Golda standing, Golda in a remembered ball-gown. A small flutter of pages covered in pencil drawings gathered at his feet. He picked them up and studied them. One or two nearly hit the mark. Not Golda to the life, but close.

He started to draw again, carefully now, calling on his memory to fill out subtle details. As he worked he felt his heart swell in his chest with excitement and anticipation. He was getting closer, he could feel it. He held up the new images to catch the light.

Golda was in the doorway, a plate in one hand and a mug in the other.

"Sammy, what have you been up to? Do you know what time it is?"

Sammy checked his watch.

"It's gone two. I brought you a sandwich."

Sammy felt the pangs of hunger now. He hoped that was coffee in the mug. He took the proffered plate.

"When you've done, you'd better come in and get ready. We promised to go to Estelle and Charlie this afternoon."

That night, in bed, Sammy reflected on those sketches. He tossed and turned and longed for sleep but something about the sketches troubled him. He had been so close when Golda had appeared. It's just that he wasn't sure what he was exactly close to. There was something 'right' about his drawings but they still lacked something, something indefinable. Then it came to him, there was no flesh on the bones. The sketches lacked feeling, they lacked tangibility.

Then it came to him. They needed colour and they needed texture. He needed to paint those images. Sammy turned on his side and snuggled up to Golda's sleeping form.

The next morning, breakfast finished and coffee drunk, Sammy sat in front of a fresh white canvas, ready to start work. The

114

best of his drawings, the one closest to the feeling he wanted to invoke, was propped up beside him. From the start everything seemed to flow and Sammy worked steadily into the evening. When he closed up the studio that night he felt an inner satisfaction of having captured the elusive essence of youth that he had been aiming at.

Sammy felt a keen disappointment when he looked at the canvas next morning. Sure the girl was lovely but she wasn't Golda. And he had tricked himself last night. Last night there had been something real about the painted image, something that seemed to reach out to him, to draw him into the picture. Now the image was flat and without life.

Sammy sat in the corner of the studio as far from his canvas as possible and stared into space. A small tear of frustration formed at the corner of his eye and trickled down his cheek. He must have sat like that for a couple of hours before he roused himself. He covered the canvas with a sheet and went up to the house for lunch.

It came to him over a bowl of soup. Golda made great soup. Wednesday and Thursday were the days for soup and Sammy always looked forward to those lunch times. It was an epiphany like on the road to Damascus. Sculpture. That was the way to

115

bring form to his creation. Even better, a bronze, a bronze statue. He knew exactly what form his tribute to Golda's youth and beauty would take; he could already see it in his mind's eye. Golda as the classical Venus. Even better, he would out-Venus Venus; such was the remembered beauty of the love of his life.

Was it the sin of pride? What the Greeks would have termed hubris?

Sammy had everything he needed for his great work. The boys had not stinted when they set him up in the studio. And had he not worked with metals for most of his life?

Casting a bronze, however, is not a simple or trivial task. Sammy spent many hours on preliminary sketches until he was satisfied that he had caught the image that he held in his mind. Many more hours were taken up by fashioning the wax prototype for the casting. Throughout the process, Sammy became more and more obsessed with the project. He missed meals and worked into the night. If Golda had noticed or felt neglected, she made no mention of it. Sammy was happy and that seemed to be enough for her.

Sammy sat and contemplated the wax image when it was completed. He had captured that essence of Golda's youthful beauty that had been so elusive on canvas. It was so perfect that he felt a qualm about committing it to the mould but eventually, reassured that an even more durable image lay at the end of the work, he enrobed the wax in the sand mould.

Later, when the mould was chipped away, Sammy knew he had succeeded. He had captured a fragment of youth and now he held it in his hand. His elation was almost god-like as he gazed on his creation.

He cleaned and burnished the figure with great care until it shone dully in the shaft of sunlight that angled through the studio window. He sat and looked at the figure with something like reverence and awe. He had captured her, his Golda, to the life. A life now gone by, but he had it trapped as if in aspic.

It should have been a contented and fulfilled man who settled down in bed beside Golda that night. Instead Sammy felt the pull of the little image he had created. He tossed and turned until eventually he yielded to the call. Barefoot and in pyjamas he crossed the moonlight grass to the studio.

The bronze statue was just where he had left it. He switched on a desk lamp and the figure was bathed in light. He sat and looked at it, still filled with an almost reverential awe at his creation.

He must have nodded off because it was the noise, as of a heavy object moving around the studio that jerked him awake. He was stunned by what he saw.

The bronze statue stood on the floor not six feet away from him. And it had grown! The figure now stood some six feet tall and towered over the diminutive Sammy in a threatening manner. Then he saw the face. It was no longer Golda's girlish face but the visage of an implacable goddess.

Sammy knew viscerally that he sat before the incarnation of Venus. The goddess' nostrils flared and her face bore the look of a terrible anger. Sammy knew his sin and understood the price that was to be exacted. Strangely he did not seek to flee but instead stepped towards the animate image of the goddess. It was the placatory offering of the ancients.

The goddess came forward and reached her arms about her prey, clasping Sammy to her bosom. He felt the cold, hard bronze on his skin. The pressure of metal arms increased on his torso. The tightness in his chest was growing, becoming unbearable, Sammy felt as if his heart was about to explode. The blackness came upon him.

The doctor said it was a heart attack that had killed Sammy. He noticed the bruises around Sammy's ribs but put that down to the fall onto the small bronze figure that they found underneath the body. It wasn't as if it had been unexpected. His patient had never listened to his advice. He had been living on borrowed time. Golda seemed to be taking it in her stride. There were tears, of course, but she had the boys to fall back on. Golda had been expecting something like it to happen soon. Sammy had been acting strangely for some time. He had seemed distracted and distant. It was as if he were somehow withdrawing, getting ready to depart.

The doctor was relieved that Golda was so accepting. What did strike him as strange, though, was that when he looked in at the studio for the last time, of the small bronze figure there wasn't a sign.

# THE CANDIDATE

The shaft of sunlight through the window woke the old man as it had done for many years past. Such was the routine of ages that he climbed out of his bed and was standing in the bathroom before he gave conscious thought to anything.

Something extraordinary was going to happen this day. The remembrance broke the flow of his morning ritual. It was the day that the candidate was due to come. He smiled inwardly at the comfortable thought.

The old man showered. He shaved carefully using the straight razor he had used for years. It struck him then that here was an odd case of role reversal. It was expected that the candidate should take care to make himself presentable; to make what was termed a good impression. Yet here he was investing that extra care in his own appearance.

As usual, the clothes for the day had been laid out for him in his dressing room. He looked at himself in the long mirror and thought that he still cut a handsome figure.

Breakfast had been laid in the dining room. The old man sat and ate, alone and in silence. A dispatch box of red leather had also been placed on the table awaiting his attention. He poured another cup of coffee and drew the box to him and took out the pile of documents that it contained. There were a few papers that only required a quick scan and his signature in agreement. He dealt with these quickly and replaced them in the box. There was also a thick report that would obviously require careful reading and would demand a significant response. He took this with him into his study.

There was already a pile of untouched papers on the desk. The old man sat and leafed through them before returning to the newly arrived document. He hefted it in his hand. Long experience of such things told him it held some two hundred pages. He placed it on the desk and stared into space, fixing his eye on the angle of ceiling where two corners of the room joined. He was not in the mood to tackle serious work today.

He checked his watch. The candidate was not due for some time. On another day the old man would have steeled himself, put his distaste away and got down to work. Today, however, felt like a holiday. The promise of the candidate's arrival pushed all other thoughts of work and duty to the very back of his mind.

Today should be a mere formality. If his trusted advisors had performed their tasks with their usual care and wisdom then the candidate would be the perfect choice.

The candidate's particulars were contained in a red leather folder that sat on one side of the desk. There were also reports of the several interviews he had already undergone together with assessments by the members of the ten man tribunal that he had faced. The old man drew it to him and read again the word pictures of his advisors. On paper, certainly, and by report without doubt, here was the perfect man for the position.

There was a photograph too. It could have been the old man's own image from forty years before. A handsome man, in the prime of life. He had the look of a serious young man. Maybe it was the spectacles or possibly the lightly furrowed brow.

The old man closed the folder and sat back in his chair. There was no way in which he would be able to settle to work. This coming meeting was too important and too much hoped for, to permit him to turn his attention to other matters. He started to pace the room, stopping occasionally to stare out of the window at the cityscape that was spread out many floors below him.

He realised that he was consumed with nerves. He felt his muscles become tense and his hands start to tremble involuntarily. Of course! It had been many years since he had stood face to face with another human being. The servants who looked after his daily welfare were never in the same room as he. His daily needs and his sometime requests all appeared as if by magic and without human agency.

If he had wanted company he had only to make his desires known and a suitable companion would have been supplied. Once he had felt the need for the presence of another person and had made his wishes known. He had not felt such a need for many years now. So, in complete isolation, he had read the reports supplied to him with monotonous regularity, expressed his need for clarification or further information in writing and had eventually handed down his decisions in documents sealed with his signet.

He had lost track of time when the sound of a soft chime announced the arrival of the elevator that served the old man's suite of rooms atop the tower. The candidate had arrived.

The old man stepped into the drawing room just as the elevator door opened and the young man who he knew to be the candidate stepped into the room. With great assurance he advanced towards the old man and held out his hand. The old man hesitated for an instant before he recalled the long unused protocol and took the proffered hand in his own.

"You are Michael?"

"Yes, your majesty," and the young man was about to bend the knee before the old man with a hand under his forearm raised him up.

"No need for all that, Michael."

"Thank you, your majesty."

"And there's no need for that either. We need to talk, so let's be informal. Better just call me George," and he gestured for him to take a seat.

The old man, who was indeed both King and Emperor, took a seat opposite and cleared his throat.

"You know, Michael, you are the first of my subjects that I have spoken to in thirty years."

The young man seemed perplexed. He cleared his throat and sought for an appropriate response. The king motioned for him to take a seat and sat opposite him.

"Forgive me. Of course you wouldn't be aware of the arrangements..."

They sat in silence as the king scrutinised the younger man. Then,

"I suppose you must have seen quite a bit of our country?"

Michael agreed that he had indeed travelled widely and was familiar with the landmarks, historical and commercial, of the land.

"Tell me," the king pursued, "have you seen the new dam? What did you think of it? What is it actually like?"

Michael again seemed to find the question somewhat strange and couldn't help remarking that he thought that the king would know what it was like having officiated at the opening ceremony just a few weeks before. This brought a smile to the king's lips and he nodded to himself.

"I apologise once more. I should explain. It is, after all, pertinent to the position we are offering. You see, I never leave this apartment. I haven't been down there," and he motioned to the outside world," in forty years."

"But I saw you opening the dam...on the newscast."

"Ah yes. It is necessary to keep up the pretence of my being about in the country...to reassure the populace. All done with computers and such like. You see many years ago, before my time in fact, a form of government was evolved that called for the complete separation of the head of state from the elected representatives of the people. It was a defence against corruption. The only way my ministers communicate with me is by written report and recommendation. I never see them so they cannot exert undue influence on me by way of personal charm or affection."

"Amazing! So you never go outside or speak to anyone?"

"There's a terrace – I'll show you later – I don't lack for fresh air, if that is your concern. I could also ask for companionship but I've got out of the habit. Believe me it all works rather well. Come along I'll show you around."

The next hours were occupied with a tour of the extensive apartment. King George showed Michael the candidate through the rooms until they reached the study where they sat for some time as the king cross-questioned him on all aspects of his life, experience and opinions. By the end of this interview the old man was completely satisfied that here was a man fit and capable for the task ahead.

"Let's go out onto the terrace," the king suggested and led the way. Champagne and glasses had been placed on a table in anticipation and George offered the young man a glass. When they were seated he raised his glass in token of a congratulatory toast.

"Well, Michael, you've done very well. I think you would suit the position admirably."

The young man allowed himself a smile of relief. It is always nice to be told that you have been successful, however at no time had the king or any of his ministers been specific as to the duties he was to be asked to perform. He had assumed that some discreet office of state was to be the reward for surviving the intense session of interviews and had refrained from asking for clarification lest that be seen as a lack of whatever quality was required. Now, however, he could not hold back.

"Thank you George. I'm glad that you think I'll be suitable for this post. Can you be specific about the duties – no-one seems to have stated what will actually be expected of me..."

"Ah, I thought I'd been through everything in great detail."

"Yes, George – you've spoken in depth about your own function and how you are constrained to live in these apartments. But what post are you offering me?"

"Why, to be my successor! All hail King Michael!" and the old man raised his glass again.

Michael was horrified and staggered to his feet.

"You can't be serious. Why would I want to...?"

"Live like this? Duty, Michael. Duty, pure and simple. You have the character and the intellect. You were born to be king."

With that the old king got to his feet and walked to the edge of the terrace. He looked back at Michael briefly then swung his legs over the safety rails and launched himself into space.

Michael was rooted to the spot for an instant then ran to the spot where the old man had disappeared. He looked down but the tower was too tall and he could see no sign of the crushed body of the erstwhile king.

All he knew then was that he had to escape from this awful place. There was no way that he was going to spend the rest of his life as a prisoner of kingship, deprived of real human contact.

He ran through the rooms until he reached the steel door of the elevator that had brought him here. In vain he sought for the control panel that would summon the lift. He banged on the doors and yelled for release. He clawed at the edges of the doors until his finger nails bled. The elevator doors remained impervious and sealed.

He looked about him in the gathering silence of the apartment. His breathing settled. He knew himself to be completely alone but observed. There was no option. He had been chosen. It was his duty.

Heavily he walked to the study and sat in the red leather chair in front of the desk. He took up the thick report, weighed it in his hand and began to read.

# MISTER METCALFE'S JOURNEY

His bag stood ready by the front door. He had packed it the night before. It was like him to be ready in advance. It had not taken long; the necessities of life are stripped to the bone at this time and do not afford room for sentimentalities.

He sat at the table in the kitchen and consumed his habitual breakfast. Finished, he washed the bowl under the running tap, dried it carefully and returned it to its place in the cupboard. He took the last of the rubbish from under the sink and added the still damp drying cloth and the wash cloth to the bag. He placed it in the bin outside and closed and locked the garden door.

He switched off the electricity and gas from the mains points under the stairs and, taking up his case let himself out of the front door. He pulled it shut smartly and posted the key back through the letter box.

Walking through the deserted early morning streets he reflected on how all departures seemed to require an early start. A time when no-one else was about. Better, he thought, than waiting around for half a day in an idleness forced by anticipation.

He walked through the echoing and empty booking hall and onto the platform. The morning air was crisp but not unpleasant. The train that was routinely never on time arrived this morning at exactly the scheduled hour and minute. Mister Metcalfe climbed into the empty carriage and settled himself into a corner seat. He would have to change at Birmingham for the train to London but now he could relax and let his mind drift as the pleasant green countryside rolled by.

London. He hadn't been back there for twenty years and yet at one time he had thought of himself proudly as being a Londoner. The city was a place for the young, however, and he had become tired of the constant rush of people and their noise. When he had retired to his rural heaven he had truly shaken the dust of the city from his shoes and had enveloped himself in the quiet and solitude as if cuddled in a warm blanket. And now, here he was, making his way back to his roots.

It must have changed. Cities were in a constant state of change. Mr Metcalfe speculated on the differences he might find. Would he be entering some alien land where once he had been a native? The centre would be very different. This he knew from the television. Always new buildings were changing the skyline. But where he was heading – would that be so different?

It had still been a village when he had first known it but already the arms of the city had been reaching out to embrace it. While he lived there as a boy change was already taking hold. New people had arrived bringing new sights and sounds and smells. Would he recognise the place? Would much of what he remembered still exist?

Birmingham arrived while his mind was still engaged with these musings. Mr Metcalfe changed platforms and settled into the London bound train. A fast journey now that the line had been improved after years of promises and prevarication. He closed his eyes.

There had been a girl. Pretty in an unremarkable way but joyful and full of life. That was university days when there had been so much promise, so much to come. They had stayed in contact for a while then she had had the offer and gone abroad to work. Mr Metcalfe had followed his own path, never quite sure of where he intended to arrive.

Other friendships had come and gone. Opportunities presented themselves. Some were seized others ignored. Looking back on it all, nothing much of great consequence had been lost by his failure to grasp the chances offered nor by the efforts to seize those he had pursued.

Except for Dora. Meeting Dora, loving Dora, being with Dora. That was where his life took on meaning. Then she was gone after too few years.

The train arrived in London and Mr Metcalfe plunged into the stream of people hurrying along the platform and down to the Underground. Some things didn't change – the smell of dust and rubber and trapped and over-heated air still hung in the tunnels of the Underground. The clatter of the approaching train was still the same. And the journey out to the outlying suburbs would never, could never change.

At the terminus, now above ground, Mr Metcalfe stood blinking in the late afternoon sunlight. He could take a taxi to his final destination but there was no hurry. He joined the sparse queue at the bus-stop and climbed aboard the familiar double-decked red bus when it arrived. He smiled inwardly when he saw that the route number was unchanged after all these years. Still the 81B that he had taken with his mother every Saturday on the shopping expedition into the town.

Mr Metcalfe sat on the top deck and looked out at the row of housing that had sprung up on the green market-garden fields he remembered. He noticed one of the road house pubs from the thirties had been turned into a fast food restaurant. He pondered if that was the correct term for such places as the bus rumbled along.

Roundabouts were negotiated. Another landmark road house pub he saw had disappeared to be replaced by what the hoarding described as luxury one and two bedroom apartments. Then he saw the familiar sight of the public library. Straightaway he recalled the place's particular smell of wood polish, dust and paper. He smiled remembering how the librarians called his father by his first name and kept books aside for him.

The bus came up to Mr Metcalfe's stop. All he had to do was step off the bus and walk down the avenue to be at his destination in but a few minutes. Instead he felt the need to prolong this pleasant experience and he kept his seat as the bus started off again heading westward. They passed the parade of shops at the top of the avenue. Mr Metcalfe was pleased to see that the structure of faux medieval turrets remained untouched. The shops too were still there. Some in fact, including the pharmacy which had been run by kind Mr Dunn the chemist, were unchanged and performing their same function. Others were now sadly turned over to other traders.

At the next stop he got off and was stunned to see that the pub he had expected to see had disappeared and in its place yet another fast food emporium and the concrete span of its carpark. He was saddened momentarily as he remembered the childhood days when he stood outside The White Hart drinking lemonade while he and his father watched the lorries heading westward on the arterial road. His father had always liked lorries. Oddly the sadness passed and was replaced by a warm softness as he recalled those times. Whenever he thought of his father now it was usually with a mixture of regret and loss. Mr Metcalfe stood and remembered the man for whom librarians kept back books, the man who made friends everywhere, a generous man, a comforting presence.

Mr Metcalfe turned away from the fast food restaurant and strolled past the shopping parade. Here was where the butcher always performed his disappearing milk trick for a small boy. Here the radio and bicycle shop where he'd been bought his first bike and a pair of roller skates. He'd never taken to either. That must have disappointed Dad who was bike mad.

He turned down the avenue. It was narrower than he recalled. Shorter too. He reached the house in no time. It was still there but the garden had disappeared under a layer of concrete. The garden that his grandmother tended with obsession.

Mr Metcalfe was not surprised to find that the front door stood ajar. He knew he was expected and entered the small hall. Inside the house was exactly as it had figured in his memory for all these years. He climbed the stairs and stood on the landing.

All of the doors stood open and he could see clearly into each room. The box room which had served as a kitchen was still as he remembered it. He entered the room at the front of the house that had been both sitting room and bedroom for his parents. Glancing out of the window he was not surprised to see that the garden had now been restored to its former state. The grass which replaced the concrete hard stand was now freshly mown. The mulberry hedge along one side had likewise been recently clipped.

Mr Metcalfe walked slowly into the next room. His room. The single bed was there along one wall, ready made up with blankets and the candlewick cover he had always remembered. There was the desk, made particularly for the grammar school boy.

Mr Metcalfe took off his shoes and lay down on the bed. He folded his hands on his stomach and closed his eyes.

Life's irony is that its end is always in its beginning.

# I'LL NEVER LEAVE YOU

It's what you say when you're deeply in love isn't it? It's what you want to hear too. You want to believe that despite every uncertainty you and your beloved will be together forever.

That was the way it was for us, for Claire and me and we both said it often, like a sacred mantra.

We were on the threshold of life. We were just starting to see the fruits of our endeavours and we were in love. My play had just opened in the West End to rapturous reviews and the advance bookings seemed to be set fair for a long run. The management had even asked for – no, demanded – a second play and I was both hard at work and caught up in the social round.

Claire too was enjoying success as a set designer and she was very much in demand.

It couldn't last though, could it? Claire was taken suddenly ill and it was all over in a matter of days.

I was devastated of course and shut myself away, barely emerging from our London apartment for weeks on end. I was fortunate however. I had friends who rallied round and a management who wanted their play and I wasn't going to be let stew for any longer than they deemed appropriate.

I pulled myself out of the pit in which I had wallowed and got back to work. It was therapeutic and healthy and it got me back on my feet. I still mourned my lost happiness but life or at least an outward image of life, carried on.

Eventually I delivered the second play and it was this that put me on the road to a full recovery. That and meeting Amanda.

The time must have been right of course. I had grieved enough and the work on the new play had somehow revitalised me and given me a new interest in life and the future. In short I was ready to re-join the world.

We took things slowly at first. I think Amanda was wary of somehow being expected to replace a memory and this made her tentative. By the time the play went off on tour however we were together and she had moved in with me.

I had bought the cottage as a bolt-hole for Claire and me. It was close to the sea on the edge of a village that nestled in the rich Norfolk farmland. It was intended as our escape route from the hurley-burley of the London theatrical scene – a place to relax and focus on each other. It wasn't to be of course.

I hadn't so much closed the place up after Claire's death as forgotten about it. Even that's not quite true. I suppose I had pushed any thought of the place to the dark recesses of the mind. I had had no desire to go there. It was a special place that was special no longer. Then one morning the place came into my mind and I was seized by an urgent desire to go there.

Why not? It was a delightful place. Amanda deserved a little holiday. So did I for that matter. It now seemed ridiculous to leave the place to rot. It could be a delight for Amanda and me. It could be our retreat.

We drove down one Friday in early autumn. The weather was crisp with just a hint of the coming winter. I was excited to be showing the place to Amanda and taking her to explore the surrounding countryside and to showing her the view from the cliffs above the North Sea. I was also nervous about the state in which we might find the place. It was probably draped in cobwebs and freezing cold.

I need not have worried. The front door was not locked and a healthy fire was in the grate to welcome us. The whole place was warm and inviting and looked to have been freshly cleaned. I blessed Mrs Dawes, my nearest neighbour for her thoughtfulness. I assumed that she must have stepped in to look after the place during my prolonged absence. It must have been her hand that had laid and lighted the welcoming fire.

We made ourselves at home. There was tea in a kitchen cupboard and we brewed a cup and warmed ourselves by the fire. Just as we were considering a trip to the local shop for provisions there was a tentative tap at the door. It was Mrs Dawes bringing a basket with a few essentials which she thought we might need.

Naturally I asked her in and offered her a cup of tea. When, however, I began to thank her profusely for arranging things in the cottage I was taken aback by her reaction. She seemed flustered and denied that she had had anything to do with cleaning the place or setting the welcoming fire. She even claimed complete ignorance of our visit, saying that she only knew we were there when she saw us drive up the lane and park outside the cottage.

I put it all down to her natural reticence. People thereabouts are very inward looking. It was possible, I reasoned with myself, that she was anxious that she had somehow overstepped the mark by her kind and generous action. I decided to let the matter rest, thanked Mrs Dawes for her basket of provisions and let her depart back down the lane.

Later that evening a storm blew in off the sea. The wind whipped around the little cottage with us snug inside. It felt safe.

Then the phone bell tinkled. Not a full blown ring you understand, just the faintest movement of the bell. I assumed it had something to do with the wind disturbing the overhead wires but when it persisted I lifted the handset.

At first I just heard the usual static of an open telephone line. Then there was a voice, very faint as if from long way away. I froze. The voice was Claire's and she said 'I'll never leave you.'

With a trembling hand I replaced the receiver. I stood in silence looking at the phone until Amanda asking who was calling brought me back to reality. I brushed off her query with some explanation about a malfunction of the line due to the storm. I suppose I probably believed it myself at the time.

I was shaken though. I tried my best to hide it. I poured myself a healthy measure of scotch and settled back by the fire. The tinkling bell had stopped and didn't disturb us for the rest of the night.

The next day was bright and clear, the air scrubbed clean by rain and scouring wind. I was alone in the sitting room when the tinkling bell started again. I grabbed up the receiver. There was the same static on the line and then the voice, less distant and a degree louder. 'I'll never leave you.' It was unmistakeably Claire.

I held the phone to my ear for several minutes, stunned by what I was hearing. I replaced the receiver and just sat, looking at the instrument. My mind was a jumble of thoughts and the pit of my stomach was churning.

I tried to make sense of what had happened. The nearest I came was to suspect a practical joke in the very poorest of taste. But I could think of no-one who might stoop to such an act of viciousness.

Over the next few days the tinkling continued to occur. I tried to ignore it when I was alone. When Amanda was there I felt constrained to pick up the receiver. The voice was always the same just a little closer each time, a little clearer. The message was always the same, 'I'll never leave you.'

I almost couldn't bear to be in that room and started to find excuses not to linger there. I'm sure Amanda noticed.

Then I began to see her. This was outside the house, at first. We'd be in the nearby town and I'd just glimpse the familiar figure out of the corner of my eye and when I turned to look she was gone.

Then the sightings, if I can call them such, became more distinct. There she was sitting at the next table in the café. We'd stop off at our local pub for drinks. There she was in the darkest corner and she was watching me. Soon I began to hear, in my head, the old familiar refrain, 'I'll never leave you.'

It got worse. She was in the house. I'd walk into a room and she'd be there. She'd linger a few seconds – just long enough for her familiar message to play in my head, and then she was gone. She was cunning too. She always chose her moment; always when I was alone.

Amanda must have been aware of something amiss. I was becoming irritable, small things would upset me all the time. She didn't say anything but I felt her wariness, her watchfulness. I should have confided in her but how to do that without sounding like I was going out of my mind.

Then, at the weekend, we had settled down to listen to a radio play in which Amanda had a good part. The action of the piece was well underway when very clearly and distinctly from the radio speaker came the voice I now dreaded and the familiar message, 'I'll never leave you.'

I looked at Amanda, horrified, she must have heard it. She seemed totally unaware, still engaged with the broadcast.

Again Claire's voice erupted from the radio. 'I'll never leave you.'

I ran from the room. In the bedroom the voice followed me. Again and again those awful words, 'I'll never leave you,' throbbed in my head. I seemed to be surrounded by Claire's voice, repeating those same words again and again, the volume increasing until my ears ached. I felt the world closing in on me, my legs gave under me and mercifully oblivion claimed me.

They brought me straight here or so I'm told. I was raving for several days before I returned to the world and during that time I lived a nightmare of which, mercifully, only fragments remain.

I like it here. It feels safe. And when she comes there's always someone I can call and they come straight away with my medicine.

Oh yes, she found me again. She found me here – probably came right along with me. She wants me to join her you see. I'd promised never to leave her and now she wants me.

It's nearly her time now. If I were you I'd go. I can't you see, but you should. It's never pretty. That's right but do come again...

# TELLER OF TALES

On the sales blurb it said that Stevenson (Robert Louis that is) had used one just like it. He carried it with him, a constant companion. They had called him "Tusitala", "Teller of Tales", in Samoa. I'd always thought that that was a wonderful thing to be called.

I didn't think that owning one would make me into Robert Louis, but I wanted to be a teller of tales and I had one to tell. I had nursed it for years. I had stroked it in the dead of night before sleep claimed me.

Now it was ready to come out. The years of gestation were ended. I knew it. The tale was struggling inside me and demanding to be told.

It was fragments though. I needed to capture them. Pin them. Put them in order. Connect them. Those fragments, they popped out at inconvenient times. Then they escaped, like feathers in a wind or gossamer disappearing in the light of day.

Then when I sat at the computer screen nothing came. That when they hid themselves and refused to come out.

I paid over my money and slipped the slim black volume into my pocket. Now I had a constant companion there at my fingertips. A repository for my thoughts.

A repository, that's me. A repository of thoughts and memories. Of things that have been, of things that might be, of things that may never be. I hide the mundane, the shameful, the awesome and the terrible.

I am dangerous. You must be careful how you use me. Keep me close and guard me. Remember, a secret is a secret when only one mind holds it. Be careful when you confide in me.

It was a mistake on his part. Or was it? Did he want to reveal himself? Was this the only way he could find?

The woman never existed. She was all just imagination. He had a vivid imagination. He had a graphic inner life.

He wrote. That's how he made a living. History mainly, that was his day-job. He was a teacher, a history teacher. The text books he turned out were a good earner, they supplemented the basic salary. That's what bought all this, the nice house, the place in France.

He aspired to other things. He wanted to write fiction. Everyone has a novel in them, isn't that right? He was just trying to let it out.

He was careless that was all. He was always leaving things about. But then what did he have to hide? Maybe he had wanted her to see it, to share his thoughts and motivations.

She didn't see a work of fiction. She took it for solid fact.

Now the blank pages are stained and no-one will write another story on them. The story is there for all time, stained in red.

Printed in Poland
by Amazon Fulfillment
Poland Sp. z o.o., Wrocław